INTERTWINED

by

Carole L Curry

Get the Free Devotional

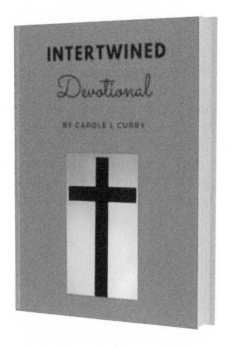

Go to www.creationsbycarolecurry.com to get your free Devotional.

This book is dedicated to all my loving and supportive family, especially my dad, Leonard Reeves, my husband Dallas Curry, and my children: my joy and my gift from God.

It is dedicated to the memory of my mother Suzanne Reeves who gave me the gift of my faith; my Uncle Dennis Steele who helped it broaden; to the sisters at the Abby of St Walburga in Virginia Dale, CO who have helped my faith blossom; and anyone who has not found a spiritual home, may you find your faith family somewhere, someday.

Author's Note:

In Roman Catholic doctrine, heaven, hell, and purgatory are states of mind rather than physical places, and they are states we already put ourselves in during our lives on Earth. Similarly, in the beliefs of the Church of Jesus Christ of Latter-day Saints, spiritual paradise and prison are also states of mind. I have found that humans often create the physical places we need in our own minds even when we are no longer there. The human imagination knows no limits in what we create to punish ourselves and to heal ourselves.

Table of Contents

So then, confess your sins to one another and pray for one another, so that you will be healed. The prayer of a good person has a powerful effect.
James 5: 16

Chapter 1

"I confess to almighty God
and to you, my brothers and sisters,
that I have sinned through my own
fault
in my thoughts and in my words,
in what I have done,
and in what I have failed to do"

Roman Catholic Penitential Rite

CATHERINE

Where do you begin when you're talking about death? Especially when it's your own. The experience after death isn't completely beyond comprehension, at least not all of it. For me, this journey starts on a sunny day that should feel warm and pleasant. Instead, it is cold and empty in a sterile hospital bed. I know the end is coming when the pain stops. It heralds the beginning of the end.

For as long as mankind has existed, we have stared at the stars and wondered what's out there. What's next? Early on we laid our dead in caves and tombs, longing to see their smiling faces: the comfort of an absent mother's hug, the warmth of a lover's embrace, the laughter of a child lost too soon. We hope that we will see them again; that there is someplace beyond the cold touch of death. Someone who transcends this painful existence, watching, guiding, loving. Some say we create religions out of a world of fantasy. Some fantasies contain a Truth beyond what we see and know around us. Some Truth cannot be known until it is experienced; it is like the wind rushing around you. You cannot grasp it in your hand, no matter how hard you try. I can tell you there is something and someone out there.

BRICE

My whole life, I have always known what I can expect after death. I spent every Sunday at church with my family, then on my own path as an adult. Bible study after Bible study, lesson after lesson, prayer after dutiful prayer, service after service furthering my progression into understanding and knowing God's love more deeply. I have never had any doubt about what would come.

My death, on the other hand, is lonely and ugly. I am glad I am alone in the car. I don't want my family to suffer as I do now. Nor do I wish for them to witness my agony. Still, the isolation of my end on Earth is deafening. I wish to hold my sons as tears well in my eyes. I long for one last kiss from my wife. My only solace is the hope that I'll see my daughter again, bittersweet though it would be. This isn't how my life is supposed to end.

I am driving home late. '*I should be there already,*' I think, looking at the time on the console. I don't see the other car run the stop sign until it is too late. There is a blinding light and sudden screeching of breaks; a series of bangs as the vehicles collide and crunch; as the airbag explodes in front of me; as my car hits something else beside me; the sickening sounds of metal and bone crunching. There is darkness all around me and yet the blinding light remains. I blink frantically, trying to get my eyes to adjust, but every direction I look is different and confusing. There is a ringing in my ears and a deep empty silence all around. Then I see him, and next, the other car. I raise my arm to shield my eyes from his headlights. I didn't know him, but now I do. I burn his face into my memory to tell the police. He jumps back into his car and drives away. I check my pockets for my phone. I check the seat, nothing. I try the door handle, but it doesn't budge. I look out the window beside me and I see tree bark very close to it. My car is pinned against the tree. I'm trapped. All alone. I call out for help. I yell. I scream until my voice is hoarse; and then, I weep.

I am not the one who is drinking and driving. I am not the one who commits the sins, but I am the one to suffer for them. I don't know how long I sit trapped between my blinding headlights and the inky abyss around me. Alone in the cold, dark night, I can't help that my last thought is, '*Why, oh why God, have you abandoned me?*'

Catherine

It seems as if I pass through a veil of mist, but sweeter. Almost sickeningly sweet. Is it incense I pass through? And then I am somewhere else entirely, foreign in comparison with the hospital room, yet familiar. My vision focuses a little more as the blinding light dances and settles into place; recognition dawns on me. After all, where else would I meet Jesus? It isn't really a surprise to me that the next place I go after I die is my church. It always was like going home, in the best and worst kind of way. It is where *I* am at my best and worst. This is where I found God… and my demons.

Light reflects and refracts through the stained glass in a menagerie of confusing rainbows in every direction. Some are clearly showing the reverse of their colorful depictions of saints and stories; others, a jumbled kaleidoscope of light. There are also dark shadows in places the light doesn't reach. Black inky depths of seemingly unknown spaces between the pews and among the rafters. The beams are visible above me like wooden rays stretching from the center braces that are their suns. There are statues around, most of which I am familiar with; friends when I was a lonely child. I see Mary and feel the comfort wash over me. I walk over and run my fingers along her outline. Mother of the motherless, or in my case, of those whose mother who was too human and fallible. Mine would always defensively say she was doing her best, but… at least I'd always have Mary. Firm

5

as the stone she is craft from, yet warm and lovingly kind. I can feel her holding me in my distress. I gasp, it looks like Mary… like she smiles at me. That's impossible, it's just a statue. What is impossible here though?

I turn and see the large marble altar on one side and the ambo on the other, the balance between meal and word. Both are mostly marble, looking very old and modern at the same time. The light from the windows is not the only light. Candles are scattered all around. Those I am used to seeing around the altar and also those I see scattered among the pews, statues, and windows. Each light flickering, dancing, but not wavering in their determined glow.

I walk past the baptismal font and let my fingers skim the top, sending ripples, disturbing the quiet surface. It is small, barely a basin even, simple, yet elegant. The water ripples peacefully. I can smell the flowers before I notice them. All kinds and colors, yet beautifully placed. A careful combination, each individual bloom exactly where it belongs.

The deafening silence is the only difference from the sanctuary I have known. There is no music, no voices of any kind, no laughter, no birds outside the windows, not even the wind rustling through the trees. The silence is unsettling. Chairs are neatly aligned in the back and in nooks for extra seating. The hardwood of the pews is pretty, but cold and unforgiving on your back, yet the seat is updated with a cushion for some comfort. We can't be too masochistic, not in the *modern* church. I run my hand along the back of each pew, and I am surprised at how it feels the same. Can a soul touch? I continue, caressing these familiar wood-workings until I find my favorite spot. As I sit, I begin to ponder this place more deeply. Is this where eternity ends? Some Sundays, it is where it seems to begin, but how can this be the end? The church is where you find your way to heaven, not heaven itself? And why am I all alone? Does everyone go through this? Is it all in the same church? I can't help but chuckle thinking of some of my neighbors' surprise at waking up in a basilica.

My side starts to itch. I am not sure about my clothes. What is this, a dress? A tunic, I think. It looks like it is supposed to be white, but it is stained and quite filthy. And itchy. How can it be so uncomfortable? I don't even have a body anymore. How can a fabric be itchy on a soul? I sulk a little as I run my hands from my itchy side and weave my fingers around my stomach. The fat lumps, loose skin, and stretch marks are all still there. I look down. What happened to my feet? I guess I realize shoes would be irrelevant here, but I don't think I have ever seen my feet so *dirty*. Caked with dried dust, and red stuff, is that blood? Ouch, I think there are sores on them. What did I do; run a marathon barefoot on the way to heaven? I reach for the pew to get a better look at one of my feet and I happen to glance at my arm. No! My heart sinks and tears well in my eyes. I am not supposed to have my scars and imperfections. I run my fingers down those white lines. Would I ever be free of

Theodore? Apparently not, not even in death. I thought I would be made perfect here?

I pick up the hymnal in front of me and thumb through it. Classic, almost ancient hymns alongside modern catchier tunes. Ava Maria, Amazing Grace, Hail Holy Queen, Be Not Afraid, Like the Bread, Gather Us In, Present Moment, Break My Heart. I easily find my favorite: Here in This Place.

This suddenly feels so lonely. Where are my family and friends? My daughter was just by my side. I know I heard her a moment ago. Is that her I hear again? Her crying fades. Just out of reach for me to comfort. No, I wouldn't see her yet. I got here first. My sister then, where is my sister? It is then that I realize I am not alone after all.

BRICE

I pass through a veil, almost a curtain, and am relieved to wake up in my sanctuary. Of course such a holy place would be the next step to eternity. Then why did I suddenly feel afraid? I know I lived a good life. I always tried to do what is right. This will only be a formality. There can't be that much standing in my way. I notice an empty collections basket. The chapel is dimly lit as if the lights are out, but a little sunshine is still peeking through windows. Are those candles everywhere? I see the familiar Christus statue. I walk up to it so I can see the nail marks on His hands and feet. I can't help but reach out and touch the smooth stone. It is a comfort to feel its cold surface. I am reassured by placing my fingers in the grooves of the wounds nails once pierced. Am I really such a Doubting Thomas?

On closer inspection, I find a table around the corner to the chapel, where there is a volunteer signup sheet that is bare. I see a prayer pamphlet with Moroni atop a temple bringing a smile to my face. I am home here.

I take a step back into the large room and my heart sinks as I limp from the doorway to a nearby seat. I am supposed to be made perfect here, aren't I? How can my old injury linger then? It is then that I notice what I'm wearing. A dirty tunic; this can't be right. I notice a ring on my finger still and find some comfort for a moment, running a finger along the CTR motto inscribed on the ring, but it only lasts a moment. There is something wrong with my feet too. Not only am I still limping, but they hurt. I look down and they are covered in dirt and blood. I think about heading down the hall to the bathroom, but I feel I must stay here. I sit in a pew instead. The longer I sit here, the more I notice the familiar details around me. The scent of lilies— funeral lilies—drifts through the air. A pitcher of water on a table to the right catches my eye. The white table for serving sacrament, but only the pitcher and an empty tray sit on it now. The candles instead of the typical florescent lights are the only other noticeable difference. Their light flickers, making shadows dance around the room, teasing ethereal presences that are not there.

I notice so much that I never took the time to appreciate before. The pews are a deep brown, almost red in color, firm, yet comfortable. Neutral, yet bright in their own wooden hue. Individual, yet they fit well together. The way we are supposed to be. The podium was also the same wood but now lacks the usual microphone. I guess there isn't technology here, but I suppose we don't need it anymore. The flowers are warm purples, pinks, with a hint of blue. I think I remember those bouquets. A few paintings adorn the walls, modern depictions of the life of Jesus. Each one with new depth and brightness I never noticed before. Books nestle in a slot on the back of each pew. Music I have known my whole life. I run my fingers along the cover of one. I open the book and thumb through it, letting it fall open when I see my favorites; How Great Thou Art, The Spirit of God, Come Thou Font of Every Blessing. My gaze shifts to the windows. Light is coming in and moving. It's shifting like there are tree branches just outside being tossed around in the wind.

My focus turns internal. I anxiously await my Lord. Surely, he is everything I hope for; everything I long for; everything I know Him to be. As I wait, doubt begins to creep in—No! I steady myself. Real faith does not leave room for doubt. I know with every ounce of my being that I will see God, that I deserve this. I lived a good life. I did all the right things, stayed away from all the wrong ones. So… where is He? Deep calm washes over me and I start to doze off as I wait. I murmur a few verses to myself: Matthew 25:13, 'Stay vigilant, because you do not know the day or the hour' seemed appropriate with my drowsiness. I coach myself through it again. "Matthew 25:13, 'Stay vigilant, because you do not know the day or the hour.'" I must be ready. I jerk awake again, this time from a deeper sleep. Through my confused haze, I can't quite remember where I am. It is only when I realize there is a gentle hand on my shoulder, which must have been the catalyst that ended my slumber, that I fully remember where I am and who it is I am waiting for so eagerly. I began to tremble and I cover my face in fear. It isn't possible; I can't be worthy of this presence beside me.

Chapter 2

*"Lord, I am not worthy that you should enter under my roof,
but only say the word,
and my soul shall be healed."*

Roman Catholic Mass

CATHERINE

"Catherine, I'm here child. Come sit with me,"
He says sweetly.

I don't think I have ever heard such a melodious, comforting voice. Still, I am afraid. Judgment comes after death, I know it.

"Catherine," He calls again, "do not be afraid. Come sit with me. We have much to discuss."

There it is: *'much to discuss.'* That has to be about everything I've done wrong in my life. I know I made mistakes.

Suddenly there is a hand on my shoulder. I jump in surprise, but still, the hand is as gentle as the voice. Gentle, yet... firm. Finally, I turn, slowly though. I barely get around and am embraced in the warmest, most soothing hug I could imagine. No, actually an embrace better than anything I could have imagined. As I am held, I again smell the sweet perfume of incense, yet it doesn't make my eyes water like all those times in church. I laugh to myself; maybe the incense doesn't bother my eyes because I am dead and no longer have eyes to water.

"When you're ready, we have much to discuss." Nope, not ready. Like when the alarm goes off, but the bed is just so warm and soft. I'm going to stay right here where it's warm and soft and safe.

BRICE

"Brice."

For I know you and I call you by name—no that isn't quite it...

"Brice."

I called you by name and you are mine, Isaiah 43:1.

"Brice."

A hand gently touches my shoulder as I tremble. I fall to my knees as if I'm melting into a puddle. I feel a sense of shame I haven't felt since my childhood. My father would be so ashamed, this isn't how a man acts. My father doesn't matter though. My Father in heaven is the only one who matters now, and Jesus, and the Spirit. That's it. I can forget about everyone else for a while. It is a while before I realize Jesus is sitting in front of me and my head is gently resting in his lap as I weep. This is all too much. He is too much. Yet peace and happiness wash over me even as I am filled with fear and doubt. How in the world can I get used to peace and fear, faith and doubt, happiness and sorrow at the same time?

Everything about this is overwhelming and I want it to be over and yet... I don't want to disturb this moment.

CATHERINE

It feels like I'm asleep and yet I'm not; like I'm dreaming, but it's something else...
"Catherine."
I stir and stretch, though I oddly don't feel stiff. I'm not sure why I feel the need to stretch; an old habit I guess. I'm startled when I realize there is a man next to me. Not just any man though.
"Catherine, we have much to discuss."
"I know," I sigh heavily. As I look up and catch my first glimpse, I gasp a little. I guess I didn't look at Him that closely before, but now… Jesus is somehow everything and nothing like I expected. His face is so familiar though I've never seen it before. He isn't like any painting or statue I have ever seen of Him. He has a kindness, a softness in his features. He truly is Love incarnate. And yet He has a silent strength in His features. He is not someone to trifle with. He opens his lips to speak and I tremble in anticipation and in fear. Seeing my reaction, He simply smiles instead.
I sigh. "Okay, I'm ready to atone for what I've done. I know it will take years of torment"—I gulp—"but I'm ready."
He smiles. "What do you think this is?" He asks as He gestures all around us.
"Purgatory."

"But why here? Why not a dungeon? If it's the torment you're expecting."

"I... I don't know. It's familiar I guess."

"This is where we spent a lot of time together."

There is a deafening silence. I have no idea what to say next. Purgatory is torment and suffering and...

He smiles. Wait, can He read my thoughts? Why couldn't He? He is God. Still, He waits in silence. I can't stand it.

"So how does this work? Where is the torment? I guess it's better to get it over with," I say sheepishly.

He laughs. I stare at him. Jesus actually laughs at me.

This is not the torture I was expecting.

"You still don't get it, but you will. There is no torment, though at times it seems like torture."

"I'm confused."

"Clearly."

Um ouch, I think.

"What you call purgatory is more of a... transition. It's a place of healing and growth. A time and place to let go of everything holding you back from full communion; to become all We made you to be."

I stare, a little shell shocked.

"Let me explain it this way. It's about getting rid of the imperfections, so everything else comes together. Here like attracts like," He pauses and points to the flowers by the altar, stands and walks closer to them. I follow Him and see large water droplets like the morning dew on the petals and leaves. I focus in on one droplet and

15

it is almost like I can see my reflection in it, but that couldn't be possible. Not with my eyesight... I stop myself. Maybe here it is possible. This droplet starts to move down the leaf and connect and combine with others.

"Like attracts like," Jesus repeats, "until all holiness is in one place."

He stretches out the palm of His hand to catch the droplet. Before my eyes it disappears into His hand.

"You have to let go of your sin and pain, all that is holding you back from me," He says.

"That's it? I just have to 'let go'?"

"Oh, it's not as easy as it sounds. You have to work through everything you have done and everything that has been done to you to fully accept grace. Think of your life as like being a caterpillar, and fully entering the kingdom of God is when you are a butterfly. This is the cocoon. It's a place of complete transformation. Shedding off your pain, guilt, and all your burdens from your life. It's your chance to let go and fully accept grace and love. Time is irrelevant here, as the Psalm 90:4 says, 'For in your sight a thousand years, are like yesterday that passes by, like a few hours of one night.' You could spend a day or millennia, and it wouldn't matter. Only growth matters here."

"So that's it. I 'let go,' grow or something and move on? I thought—"

"You *still* don't think you're worthy of Our love and grace," He says gently, then goes on, "Don't get me wrong, growth isn't easy. Do you think the caterpillar *likes* melting down and reshaping

16

itself into the butterfly? It's actually quite painful—" His voice quivers and a tear streaks down his cheek.

"Then why do You make it that way?"

"Because I knew all it could become." His face glows with pride.

My cheeks burn. There is no way he could think that way about me.

He smiles deeply at me and the joy of it is almost painful.

"Okay, let's get started then," I say, breaking eye contact.

"Where to start..."

Panic suddenly hits me. Everything that's been done to me. Everything. Be careful where we start—not that, don't start with Theodore. I see something move out of the corner of my eye. Wait, we're alone here... aren't we?

We're in my parents' church, though judging from the clothes, it's easily forty years ago. I spot my family, upfront and center. Though my dad could talk my mom into not sitting in the front row, we were still very noticeable in the second pew. I see my dad holding me in his arms, when I couldn't be more than a year old. Realization dawns on me from my dad's nodding head and my approximate age. I can't help but giggle even as the priest's excitement crescendos in his homily.

I turn to face Jesus, giggling, "Um, I'm not sure why—hee hee—why I need to—ha-ha..." but I can't be serious enough to finish my question.

Jesus gives me a wry smile. "It had an impact on you."

I am already doubled over laughing before it even happens, but finally, it does.

"Oh darn it! She peed on me!" my dad yells as he jumps up, startled from his slumber by the puddle now on his chest.

My mom's face is glaringly crimson with both embarrassment and fury.

"And that's why we shouldn't sit up front," I laugh. "We're just not a front pew family, but my mom kept trying."

Jesus is chuckling too as He looks at me. "It's good to laugh," He says with His expression softening. "Think of something that brought you to Me."

"To you?"

"Yes, you found Me. Often. Pick one." He smiles.

"I—well I guess—I," and before I can even explain, the scene comes into view. The abbey was remote, several miles from town, but also modern. I stumbled upon it quite by accident one day. I saw the sign and just sort of followed it. Now looking at this same place, a warmth grows inside. This is also home, in a way. I see the stream rippling and bubbling as we walk up to it and I smile. It always brought me peace to watch the water churning and racing along. Jesus joins me on the bridge and I suddenly feel as if this isn't the first time He stood beside me in this place.

"You're right, this was a good place for us to meet."

I smile in reply and turn toward the building. It is a house for 20 or so people, but when a community comes together, that is small. It is painted grey but is not a dreary building, especially in the fiery reds and oranges of the sunset. It is difficult to describe the aura of peace it emits; you simply have to experience it. We walk toward the building. It is about 100 yards ahead of us, but the walk holds a quiet reflectiveness. There is a statue of the abbey's patroness outside and a large bell for a sister to ring for their call to prayer, not that anyone here needs a reminder of their schedule. We seem to pass through the door rather than open it, but I am only mildly disturbed by the process as it is over so quickly. I am happy to be back someplace I want to be. We walk past a few sisters and one turns as if to look at us.

"Wait, can they sense us? Is this like a haunting?"

Jesus laughs. "We are all connected. Yes, some can feel the connections you cannot see, but you are not a ghost and neither am I."

"In the name of the Father..." the sisters begin to chant.

"But they can't see us?"

"No."

"Or feel us?"

"Well—"

"Not sense us, but hold my hand; Mother Maria over there couldn't hold my hand, could she?"

"No," Jesus says, firmly, but kindly, "And this isn't why we're here. What did you find here? They are some of the things you *can* take with you."

I had to stop and think about it. What was it here that kept drawing me back?

"It's an escape—but not an empty one like TV. I don't go all mindless and zone out. I—I get filled up with something here… with peace." I need to think some more; there is more, but it is difficult to describe. "And… and contentment." I just can't seem to put my finger on the right word until I do: "and love. I just love it here."

"You *feel* love here?"

"Yes, I love"—He looks at me like I've almost got it so I go on—"and I feel loved."

Jesus smiles. I do too. I'm not quite sure, but I think I just figured out something important about Him.

"It's like I found you here."

"You did and you do and you will."

"It's in Kings or something: there was a windstorm, but God was not in the wind, there was an earthquake and God was not in the earthquake, there was a fire, but God was not in the fire, after the fire there was a whisper in the quiet."

"I am in the quiet." He grins at me.

"Wait, I *will* find you here? That doesn't make sense. Am I coming back here again?"

"Yes and no. This place is a part of you already. You don't have to go anywhere to be here."

"That doesn't…" But I stop, actually that does make sense. "So you are always here?"

"I am always here and there."

"Because you're the past, present, and future?"

"In a way."

"You will always come back here, you're a part of it, and yet, you don't need to anymore." As he says this, something beautiful appears on my right arm. I see shapes, lines, colors beautifully interwoven and yet difficult to describe. It is as if my thoughts become a picture here on my skin. Suddenly something internal becomes externally visible right before my eyes.

"There *are* some things you take with you," is all He says, and we are back at the church.

"Like a tattoo?" I ask.

"Not at all," was His only reply. Then there is a silence.

I look around and see the flowers at the altar are wilting. Is that even possible here? A few candles are knocked over, smoke still streaming from their wicks. Is that a crack in the wood of a pew? What happened here? I see something moving in the shadows. Did it attack this place?

"Wait, so are we going to have to do this for every moment of my life, like everyone I've ever talked to?"

"Have a lot you need to make up for in those conversations?"

"I well... no"—I hesitate, but continue—"can't I see Jennifer though? We don't have anything unresolved between us."

"You'll see your sister when you're ready."

"That isn't fair," I say as tears well in my eyes. "It's... it's blackmail." Did I just see something move out of the corner of my eye?

"That isn't the intent."

"Well, that's what it is! You're keeping me from my sister until—what? Until I earn it?"

"That's not what I'm doing." His voice quivers a little. "We just want what's best for you."

"Jennifer is what's best for me!"

"I don't doubt you miss your sister." He seems to choose His words carefully. "We can't have discourse. We all need to be in harmony to be together."

"So this is about control. So much for free will! It has to be your way or the highway. Everything has to be *perfect*." I slam my hand down, trembling.

"It's not like that. You just have to let go. You'll see," He says with tears in His eyes.

"You keep saying that but what does it even mean?" I snap.

"It's—do you remember scuba diving?"

I pause, then say, "Yeah on my honeymoon with Tim, but what's that—"

"You looked at pretty amazing things. The fish, coral, abundant colorful life all around you. Life is like that, and you can't take the stuff with you. You can't take the fish or coral. You couldn't even take a chest of gold if you found it on the seafloor. You definitely can't take a bunch of rocks from the seabed. You'd be weighed down. You can't rise to the surface if you try holding on to everything. So you need to let it go. 'You can't take it with you' applies to a lot more than possessions. You can't take your pain with you."

"So, I'm too heavy to go to heaven, like I'm too fat or something?" I try to joke. This is too much to think about too deeply. I can't help but try to lighten it up.

"It's not that you're too burdened—or fat." He glares at me and I try to look sheepish. "You want to see your sister, but don't you want to look your best? To be your best, really, but you'll look it too."

A flash of us getting ready for a high school dance appears before my eyes, laughing and having so much fun. I'm there with her again. I always had the best of times with my sister. "Yeah," I laugh, "We were good at looking our best."

We're back at the church now.

"You need to rest."

Yes, I do.

"You have more work to do."

"I can't take much more of this." '*I can't face Theodore,*' is what I'm really thinking.

"That's why you need to rest now, my child. You can do this. It just takes time."

He sits in a nearby pew and drapes his arms across the back. I go and sit next to Him, resting my head against his chest.

"Come you who are burdened, for my yoke is light. Isn't that in Matthew 11:28?"

I chuckle and respond, "Like a child rests in its mother's arms so I rest in you, I was thinking," I smile. "I like the Psalms. That's part of 131:2, but of course, you know that."

"It makes a beautiful song," He says.

I flinch at His last words, but try to distract myself. I look around and notice that things seem amiss around the church. More flowers are wilted now, a statue is on its side, and there is definitely a pair of beady eyes behind it.

"Do not be afraid," Jesus says. "I can't recount every time we said that one. It seems to come up a lot you know."

"Is—is that a demon or something?" I ask.

"Yes, but do not be afraid. I am with you."

"You'll keep me from temptation?"

He smiles. "I'll keep you from losing yourself."

I nod but I am not sure what he means. His presence is comforting nonetheless.

I am happy, but also tired.

"We have more work to do, but rest now."

"That sounds marvelous." I lay back on the cushioned bottom of the pew and close my eyes. As they close, I see green eyes under the pew in front of me and I almost remember to be afraid.

I open my eyes again and I'm with Jennifer. It's the memory I just saw, but I'm actually here with myself and my sister. We're getting ready for something. We're in our shared bathroom, hair and makeup products scattered everywhere. I smile as I look at us laughing and playing with the makeup brushes. The younger me turns away for a moment and as Jennifer looks in the mirror, I notice a change in her face. She looks troubled. She turns to the side and puts a hand on her stomach for a second, then quickly returns to standing square with the mirror and fixing a curl in her hair.

"Did she just—why didn't I see that?" I say, stunned. I stand next to her and reach up to touch her curls, but pull my hand back when I send her hair bouncing.

Recovering, I say, "Why couldn't she see herself how I see her? She's so beautiful." My hand drops to my side as the two girls continue to fuss and play with makeup brushes and bobby pins, giggling. "I could have saved her—if only I'd seen it," I mope.

"Possibly." Jesus shrugs.

"Wait, what? Aren't you supposed to tell me there wasn't anything I could have done?" I ask.

"But that isn't true. That's what people say to absolve themselves of their mistakes." When He sees my eyes widen, He adds, "There is always something you could have done, and we'll never know if it would have changed things. You can't actually go back and change it. Some things in your life didn't go the way you wanted and that's what we're here to heal."

"But you said I can't change what happened."

"I did and I didn't say we are changing things. I said you're here to *heal*."

Back at the church, I look around as something moves in the shadows, distracting me for a moment. I turn and I see it: a cat-sized monster creeps out of the shadows. I am a little startled. "Is that a demon?" I ask.

"Yes," Jesus replies. "But don't look so worried."

"But it's a demon!" I gasp. A shadow passes over a nearby window. "What's out there?"

Jesus smiles. "Don't worry about what's outside. We're looking at what's inside."

"But..." I see another shadow, but it almost looks familiar, like an angel.

"The big battles are waged by other forces. Yes, that's St. Michael the Archangel by the window," Jesus says.

I spy a statue of the archangel across the room and wonder if that's really what he looks like. Instead I say, "So I've got my own battles." I look at the little demon.

"It's not what you think," Jesus says.

I turn and see that Jesus is standing near the steps to the altar so I walk toward Him. He takes off His shirt and ties it around His waist so I look down, suddenly very interested in the dust on the floor.

"Catherine, come here," He calls.

I look up and see He is gesturing to a basin at the steps of the altar. I go and sit obediently, though humbly. Tenderly, He removes one of my sandals and places my left foot in the basin. The water is warm and refreshing. With His hands and a cloth, He washes away the blood and dirt. He gently sets my foot on a towel next to the basin. He turns His attention to my other foot. I am amazed at the difference, both in appearance, and in how my feet feel. He places my right foot in the water and repeats the process. Soon both of my feet feel not only clean but refreshed and pain-free. After drying my feet, He returns my sandals to them and wipes His wet hand on His shirt.

"Now child," He begins, but I interrupt Him with a yawn. He smiles and walks with me over to a pew. We sit next to each other, but my eyelids are heavy. Soon, I crumple over into a heap and fall asleep with tears streaming from my eyes.

BRICE

"Brice, I'm here when you're ready," He says gently.

How could he be so patient? Perfect. He truly is perfect.

I open my eyes and blink a few times to adjust to the light. Maybe it's just my imagination, but it seems brighter now. I wonder what's next, but I am too afraid to ask. I have waited my whole life to meet my Savior but now that it is upon me, I feel so incredibly inadequate. How could I possibly deserve the grace bestowed on me? I stare at His feet, step by step until they are right in front of me. I feel a gentle touch under my chin. I close my eyes as tight as I can. The fingers gently raise my face to the light from the window. It is definitely brighter now, but not from the window. I open my eyes and am dazzled by His splendor.

He smiles and begins, "This isn't torture or torment—"

"I know," I say, then I blush. I can't believe I just interrupted my Savior.

He looks me straight in the eye, but He just smiles and continues, "It will be difficult and even painful. That's the way change is. It's not meant to be torture or even a test for you. It's like oil on the surface of water."

"It separates," I say flatly.

"Not the oil; the oil seeks out other oil until all is one." Jesus explains.

He is standing in front of the baptismal font now and there is a flask of some kind in His hand. He pours oil, olive oil from the look and smell of it, on top of the water. I watch as blobs of oil collide and combine getting bigger until He has poured out so much oil there is an even layer of it above the water. '*How much of Himself must He pour out like this?*' I wonder.

"All of myself," He answers my thought, "But for a good reason. For the best reason. I want you to become what you were always created to be, perfect."

I am about to protest until I hear that last word. My mouth snapped shut. Perfect; no one could argue with not being perfect.

"Shall we begin?" He asks.

At a loss for anything more eloquent to say, I reply, "Sure." Yeah, I'm off to a great start; very impressive.

"What brought you to me?" Jesus asks in response.

I always knew there was a God, I think to myself, but it was never as clear as the day Peia was born. We knew she was going to be different; I didn't expect her to be perfect. I admit she had me wrapped around her little finger from the very beginning. She was Daddy's little girl and I would never have asked for her to be anything else.

I see myself holding her tiny form as she cries and coos at the wonderment of this new and frightening world around her.

"Don't worry, Daddy's here," I coo back at her.

The joy of holding her in my arms at last and now… If only I could hold her again. I'm dead and so is she, so where is she? I wish to hold my sons again as tears well in my eyes. I long for my wife. Right now, I just need to focus on Cassiopeia, but where is she? When will I be reunited with her?

Instead we are in a memory of mine. I'm around fourteen from the look of me. I am just entering the dining room and straightening my tie. My brother is sixteen and I already want nothing to do with him.

"Bryan, are you coming?" my mom asks him when she enters the room in her dress and heels, still adjusting her earrings.

"No," he simply says from the living room couch. No explanation, not even any excuses.

"Let's go, Brice," she turns to me.

"But—" I start to say.

"Let's go," she says sternly.

"I'll never get that," I say to Jesus, "was she trying to make me the dutiful and jealous son? Bryan was clearly the prodigal one!" I fume, "I mean it never even mattered to her when I tried, so why did I even bother!"

"What did you get out of going with her?" Jesus asks.

Without any good retort, I snap, "Nothing."

Jesus smiles, and I feel like I'm missing the point.

I'm back at the church but something seems different. I can't quite place it, but something— something's missing. I was never that good at details though, so I can't figure out what.

Jesus is still standing beside me.

"So that's it?" I ask Him.

"For now. Things like this take time. This can be a place to rest and find yourself again."

As if I could lose myself.

Wait, did I just see something move in the corner? When I look over, there's nothing there. That's strange.

Something is off again. The pews—the pews look worn and tattered. The carpet! The first time it was the carpet. It looks worn and dirty now too. Is that an animal under one of the pews? What's happening to this place?

"It carries your pain too. This place, you, me, all need to heal."

I could never imagine such a holy place in such disrepair; it's unsettling. Just then, stuffing pops out of a nearby seat and I gasp.

'*This is all so overwhelming*,' I think, when I am distracted by movement in front of me. Little, beady green eyes appear in a shadow.

"What are those?" I wonder aloud.

"Your demons, of course," Jesus replies. "We all have or have had some to work through."

I think about our messages every Sunday: be more like God, find the impurities, your demons, and find the ways to get rid of them. Chose the right way, the way to God. How did my demons end up here though? I always found the good around me, or so I thought.

"So those little gremlins are my demons? They aren't so bad." I'm staring at one peeking out from under a pew in front of me. I sit in the pew and lean over to get a better look. "They're almost cute." It yawns and stretches as a cat would. I almost expect the demon to pounce on me for calling it cute, but it just stares at me intently. What does it want?

My soul, of course, I remind myself and I stiffen.

"Why are they here?" I say out loud instead.

"They," Jesus explains, "are a part of you."

"Me?" I say taken aback. "That… that can't be a part of me!"

"That one," Jesus points at the green-eyed one in front of me, "is your jealousy."

I sit upright, stunned.

"So, it's the worst part of me," I say as I stand up and shoo it with my foot. It scurries away to a row of pews across the aisle, still eyeing me intently.

"How do I get rid of it? Do I have to exorcise it or something?" I turn to Jesus.

"You have to accept it and heal yourself," He replies.

"No, that can't be right. I… I can't, it's…" I close my eyes and rub them. "You're supposed to get rid of demons, sin, all that bad stuff. It… I can't go to heaven with a demon tagging along as a pet!"

"It won't tag along. You're not ready yet," He says, "but you will be."

A few more demons have slinked out of the shadows. These ones are larger, like mid-sized dogs but much more menacing. Their eyes are unnerving. I know I'm already dead, but I don't want to find out how those claws feel. What are they doing here anyway? It's not like I went to… I didn't, right?

"When do we get to the important stuff?" I turn from the demons, but now I can't look away from the stuffing that is still bouncing from the seat of the pew in front of me.

"It all is important."

That wasn't what I meant. I put my head in my hands, "I mean—I don't know what I mean."

"This is hard on everyone. It is also critical. One step at a time. And then we rebuild—Together."

"Okay." I look in His eyes. If this is how it has to be; this is how it has to be.

We're not at the church anymore.

"Oh, God," I gasp. It's Peia. I see her, but I don't get to hold her. I think I might cry. It's the day I lost her.

"It's okay, I'm with you. I was with you then, I'm with you now. And I will always be by your side."

Tears do fill my eyes now. "I know she's in a better place. God, I just want to be with her again."

Jesus nods but doesn't say anything.

Something in me hardens. "I've had just about enough of all this 'Ghost of Christmas past' B.S."

"I know it's hard," Jesus continues. "This isn't about Cassiopeia. Or even your grief. I know it's hard to look past your own pain, but you need to see the bigger picture."

'What could possibly be more important than the loss of my child?' "What's so important?" I seethe.

"Your pride."

I swallow hard. I see myself. I'm sitting in the hospital lobby. I stare off in disbelief. Not willing to cry. Not then.

"You ok?" a woman asks.

I know her from school. I've known her for years, but...

"Did you ever really know her though?" Jesus asks me.

"I—I can't say that I did. We didn't exactly hang around with the same people. Is that what this is about? *Her*?"

"I already told you. It's about your pride."

"I'm fine," I hear the younger me say. "She's in a better place."

"If you need to talk…" She looks down, her voice trails off without finishing the sentence.

"I'm fine." I wasn't fine. I stand up and walk away. She sits down next to the empty seat and puts her head in her hands. She's crying. Why is *she* crying? Why should I care?

"She was a nurse who tried to help save Peia. She was hurting too."

Of course, she's clearly wearing scrubs, but...

"So, her pain is more important than mine?" I snap.

"No, I never said that—"

"You never even mention how much I'm hurting, but hey, I blew off some stranger—almost stranger—I… I barely knew her, so yeah, so I didn't feel like pouring my heart out or anything."

I am quickly losing my steam. I can see Jesus' point as I watch her cry, but I don't want to face it.

"Righteous anger feels good, doesn't it?" Blood drips down his wrists to his fingertips. The last of my anger evaporates.

"I know she was just trying to help and she was hurting too. I can't imagine it feels good to lose a patient. Was—it wasn't her fault, was it?"

"No, she did all she could."

"Then why? I mean, it happens. It's unfortunate, but that's life. That's part of her job. What she signed up to deal with all the time. She knew what she was getting into," I justify.

Jesus looked down sullenly.

"I—that was too harsh. I just mean—why, was Peia special to her or something?"

"She was working here the day Peia was born. She saw her grow up, though from a distance. Peia reminded Catherine of the sister she lost."

"Did she have Down's Syndrome too?"

"No, they both had a particular twinkle to them."

I knew exactly the 'twinkle' He was referring to, but I thought that was part of her 'condition'.

"Everyone is a unique combination of traits We give them. Chromosomes only play a part in determining what comes out the most."

"I…" '*Did I even know my daughter that well?*' I start to wonder.

"Don't lose what's important to you in this process. That's not what this is about. It's only about healing. We have something to do first. Then we can talk about Peia."

We are back at the church and I notice that Jesus is seated in front of a basin of water.

"What's that for?" I ask.

He points to my feet.

"You can't—" I start.

Jesus smiles. "I think you know what my response to that is."

I walk over dutifully. It is humbling having Him wash my feet. The water is warm and soothing. The dirt and blood come off with some gentle scrubbing. He has a towel next to the basin to dry my feet, then He tenderly returns my sandals to my feet.

"Now," He says as He looks up at me, "are you ready to continue?"

That's when I notice the Christmas decorations around the chapel. I find it odd, but what isn't here? I am looking at the Nativity scene and so is Jesus.

"At the manger," He says. "At my beginning," He adds solemnly.

'*As I begin my ending,*' I think to myself.

"Yes," Jesus says.

I look around at the mess and decide where to start. I grab a pile of stuffing from a seat nearby. "Let's get to work then."

He sighs, I hate when He does that. It's clearly edged with disappointment. I should have been named Peter.

He smiles. "It's not that easy. You know this isn't just a building."

"I know. I… I just don't know what I'm supposed to be doing, so doing anything feels better than not knowing where to start."

He nods but doesn't say anything. Apparently, I'm supposed to guess what's next.

Chapter 3

*"HERE WE WILL TAKE THE WINE AND THE
WATER
HERE WE WILL TAKE THE BREAD OF NEW
BIRTH
HERE YOU SHALL CALL YOUR SONS AND
YOUR DAUGHTERS
CALL US ANEW TO BE SALT FOR THE EARTH*

*GIVE US TO DRINK THE WINE OF
COMPASSION
GIVE US TO EAT THE BREAD THAT IS YOU
NOURISH US WELL AND TEACH US TO
FASHION
LIVES THAT ARE HOLY AND HEARTS THAT
ARE TRUE"*

GATHER US IN BY MARTY HAUGEN

CATHERINE

"Catherine," I hear softly.
I rise and look at the large doors of the church.
"Catherine," I hear again faintly.

I run to the door, but it's locked. Frantically I tug at it, bang on the door and try again and again to open it.

"She's there! I hear her, she's right there!" I cry and crumble to the floor again.

Jesus softly goes over and picks my crumbled heap up from where I sit.

"No, I have to get out! I need to get to Jennifer!" I cry and pull myself out of His arms and to my feet.

"She isn't there," He says, reaching over and brushing my hair back.

"I hear her, she's right there!" I point at the door, but something isn't right about the voice I hear this time. I turn to Him. "She really isn't there?" I squeak.

"No, she isn't. You're doing this to yourself."

I crumple to the ground and cry until I think I have no more tears. Jesus sits with me, gently stroking my hair.

When I feel like a calm is settling over me, I say, "So that's it? That's grief? And now it's over?"

"Is it?"

"No it never really is, is it?" I sulk.

"What's wrong with that, my child?"

I have to stop and think. How do I explain what's wrong? "It's... it's depressing. People don't like to be around you if you're all sad and mopey like this. You've got to cheer up and put on a brave face and grin and bear it and... all that. It's just a part of life, so get over it."

"Catherine, there's no one here to put on a brave face for." He looks so compassionate and yet... sad also.

"I…" I can't, I just can't fall apart. "I thought you just said I was over it."

"Does it take one moment to erase years of longing for a presence that is no longer there?" A deep sadness fills His eyes. He continues in spite of His tears, "Grief isn't about getting over it or moving on, it's… it's about—"

"Not being consumed by the sudden emptiness." I can't believe my own audacity at this moment. He smiles, so I continue, "Life goes on and so you have to, but suddenly you're walking through life a little more alone then the day before they were gone. But you have to keep walking. Life doesn't stop… even when it does." My eyes well up. And not just for Jennifer. For my mom, my grandparents, a few aunts and uncles, every distant relative, every family friend, every neighbor, every acquaintance; every time someone was suddenly gone from my life. Some when I was little, some much later, but I still feel every absence. I believed they were going to a better place, but now that it's my turn…

"Is it really so bad to meet Me?" Jesus asks coyly.

I laugh. Yes, they did go to a better place, I'm sure of it now. I feel a lightness wash over me like I just put down something very heavy. Nothing around me seems to change, at least not that I can see, but everything feels different. For some reason, I don't feel so alone in this empty building.

BRICE

I snap to awareness still looking into Jesus' eyes. I must have been lost in a kind of reverie. It's easy to do, but difficult to explain. I take a deep breath and break eye contact as I turn away. It's too intense to stay that connected for very long.

"That's part of the problem, Brice."

"What is?" I ask, confused.

"You struggle to stay connected for more than a few moments at a time. You need more. And we need more," He replies.

"More what?" My confusion is growing, and I am feeling rather silly having to ask.

"More connection."

"I—" He's right and suddenly I know it. I'm just not exactly sure what to do about it. I mean I'm already dead, it's not like I can go out and make more friends.

"Let me in."

"I have," I say defensively. I accepted Christ long ago.

"You have to let others in to let me in."

"I—I do… sometimes." I'm sure I can think of times I've let people in. I mean what does that even mean? How much does it take to 'let someone in'?

He just smiles as lovingly and patiently as ever. "It's the 'sometimes' part we need to work on."

I look around the empty church, "So who am I supposed to let in?" I tease. "Are they at the door?"

Jesus smiles. "You're not there yet. You have work to do here first."

CATHERINE

I wake curled up on the floor. The demon is like a cat cuddled up to my chest. A few more have come out of the shadows but have chosen to lay just out of reach. Funny, I don't remember going to sleep this time.

"Are you ready?" Jesus says. "Have you rested enough?"

"I think so." I sit up and stretch. The demon also stretches and yawns. "Can I take her with?" I smile. It is like a little pet now.

"No, it's not like that. I think after you work through more of your life, you will understand better."

I'm not in the church anymore. I'm sitting on the couch next to Theodore. We're watching something on TV without really watching it. It will be okay, I know I need to face this, I can't keep avoiding it, but...

"What's on your mind?" I hear Theodore ask the younger me.

"It's nothing, just another fight with my mom," I respond.

He slides a little closer and puts an arm around my shoulder. I settle against his chest, glad to have the comfort. Then he slowly slips his hands between my thighs.

"Tell me about it," he croons.

"Not right now." My response is weak at best.

"Okay, if you don't want to talk..." He's kissing my neck and ear.

"No, I—"

"You know you're too beautiful. I can't keep my hands off you," he says into my ear.

I feel the complete opposite of beautiful. I feel empty and suddenly so alone here with him.

"I can't help myself around you," he says as he pushes me to my side so I'm lying on the couch now.

I wish I could be anything but beautiful.

My eyes blur with tears as I turn away from the scene. "You see! He corrupted even the most caring gestures! I... I need to sit down." My head is throbbing and there are spots in my vision.

"My body seems to hurt a lot for no longer being there," I complain.

"Who said it isn't there?" Jesus reaches over and takes my hand.

After being so upset, just a moment ago, it's unnerving how calm he makes me. I don't want it! I shrug away his touch without really listening to what he had to say.

"And don't tell me it's a good time to rest," I snap. I finally notice I'm not at Theodore's anymore. I rest my hands on the pew in front of me, leaning my pounding head forward.

"I wonder if it's a good time to eat something."

"Eat something? I'm dead I don't"—my stomach growls an angry interruption. Bewildered, I look over and see a table that wasn't there before. Not the stone altar at the front of the church, but a wooden dining table set for two right in the middle of one of the main aisles. It is very

41

modern looking with its sharp angles and is a little out of place among the old-fashioned pews. Quietly, I go and sit in the closest chair and wait. This isn't a time to argue or question.

I'm not sure what is on the table in front of me. Some kind of bread or pastries, but not exactly like any I have seen before. I can smell the sweetness wafting off them. I am unsure of whether to take one or wait to be offered. I don't want to be rude or ungrateful, especially not to God.

Jesus smiles and passes the platter from the center of the table. "Take and eat."

"Let me guess, 'this is your body?'" I tease.

"Something like that yeah." He winks back.

"Do we say grace or a blessing or something?"

"Every breath is a grace from Us, every breath is a blessing given back."

"Kind of a prayer without ceasing," I smile.

He scrunched his brow. "If you intend it to be. All We want is communion with you, with or without your words. If words are what open your heart, then pour them out. We only need your openness."

I still feel obliged to say something. I bow my head and begin, "Um... thank you, God, for this food... Thank you for... oh, I don't know, everything?" I chuckle, but looking up, I continue, "Nothing I can think of is good enough to cover it. I mean poets and theologians have done this for centuries and haven't gotten it right, not all of it. No words are right or enough."

"I think that was pretty well said. Nice and from the heart, ya know?" He bites into a piece of bread and nods to one in front of me.

I take a bite and my mouth bursts with the flavor. Sweet but not sugary, both satisfying and yet I yearn for more, so hearty a bite could tide me over for days. I finish it and the crumbs; I don't want to waste a morsel.

There is a warmth inside of me now. It starts deep and grows stretching down to my fingertips and toes. This isn't just any food.

"How are you feeling?" Jesus asks.

"Good. Like really good," I respond. "I probably could run a marathon now." I laugh.

He smiles. "You become what you eat. Sometimes it feels like that. Where to next?"

"Um…" Remembering the last time, I'm not sure I want to choose. "How… how about you decide?" I say meekly. Do I even have control in all this?

"Okay." Getting up, he takes my hand. "But you may not like it."

I swallow hard. "I have to face him sometime." I rise to meet Jesus standing next to me.

"That's good." He hesitates. "You need to heal before that happens though."

BRICE

It looks like the middle of my childhood, but I don't know if I can say how old I was for sure. I have a brace on my leg… again. At the moment, I am having particular trouble maneuvering my legs and crutches successfully.

In frustration, I plop back down where I had been seated and drop my crutches.

"You won't get anywhere that way," my dad snaps from the doorway.

Without a clear comeback, I glare holes in the back of his head after he enters and turns to pick up some clutter.

In the present, I look at Jesus. "Okay, so?" I mumble, "I mean I know I may not have been respectful, but…"

Jesus lovingly puts a hand on my shoulder. The gesture opens a floodgate of emotions in me. "I—"

But Jesus interrupts, "This is where you are, who you are. You don't need to apologize for that—to anyone."

I lean against the wall and look down at my leg resentfully. "Will I ever be normal?"

Jesus turns to stand beside me. "You were made the way you have always been meant to be."

My head drops. '*So I'm cursed,*' I think, but Jesus continues, "I was never very normal either." His lip circles into a half-smile. "Normal is so boring anyway."

I lighten a little but look doubtfully at my leg. "But you heal people," I whisper to Him.

He smiles, looking at me intently. "I bring out what is already inside."

I gasp as my leg begins to tingle and I feel the muscles spasm and twitch.

"Don't get too excited," Jesus remarks. "You're still the same abnormal you," He jests, "and healing takes time."

We're back at the church now. There is a table in the front like a sacramental Sunday, but it has two chairs and no tablecloth.

"So… now we're eating?" I say, turning to the table set for two.

"Yes. You need strength to continue your journey."

Jesus walks up to the table and lifts a cup of water.

"You know I turned this stuff into wine once?" He jests with a half-smile.

"I don't—" I protest.

Jesus laughs. "I know. Water. Wine. Blood. No difference here, but this is just water."

My stomach turns a little, but I know what He means.

"How about this?" He waves a hand at the plate of some kind of bread. "Join me?" He asks.

Clumsily, I sit at the table. It seems out of place. It's too… old fashioned, with hand-carved ornate touches to the wood. The plate of bread is at the center of the table, but I try to act like I don't notice it. It would be rude to ask and even worse to help myself.

"Help yourself," Jesus says, sitting down across from me.

I'm still a little hesitant, but I take one off the top of the neat pile. It's not quite what I expected, but smells amazing. The little imperfections show it was clearly made by hand, making it even more beautiful.

"Like all of creation," Jesus smiles, finishing my thought out loud.

"So you hand make this for everyone?" I ask. I know He's omnipotent, but this seems tedious and a lot of work. I mean for *everyone*?

"This table was set and ready for you since before all creation was made." He waves his hand to the plate. "Take and eat."

I take a bite that bursts with flavor. It has a spice to it that surprises me. This is not ordinary bread. There is an aroma of wildflowers as the bread is broken open. It is like nothing I could have expected. I look down embarrassed. I am clearly overreacting. Silently, I continue eating. After I finish my first piece, Jesus hands me another. Then another. Wordless, this continues until I couldn't possibly take another bite. I sit back and the unthinkable happens. I let out a long deep belch. My face burns a deep crimson as I try to hide behind my hands.

I hear a rumble across the table. Oh no, now I'm in for it. The rumble grows into… into a chuckle, then from a deep belly laugh into a high squeal. A smile breaks across my face and I chuckle too. Soon we are slapping each other's arms across the table leaning over it in our merriment. Tears are again streaming down my cheeks. Neither of us wants to break the joy even as the laughter subsides. We sit and smile. I know there are things that need to be done, yet still, we sit and smile.

Something pulls at my pant leg, but I just shoo it with my foot. This is…

"Love, yes. I am love. And I am deeply in love with you."

Again, something pulls at my leg and scratches a little. Then…

"Ouch," I yell, "it bit me." I look down in surprise to see large green eyes far too cute for a demon. "Go away," I yell at it as I kick out. "You're ruining everything!"

A tear appears on its cheek before scurrying away on far too many legs for a cat-sized creature. It sits on a chair and looks back at me sadly like it just wants to be loved too.

"Really?" I roll my eyes.

I look back at Jesus expecting the moment to be ruined, but he still smiles lovingly.

I don't want this to end, but anxiety shakes me out of it.

"What's next?" I ask timidly.

Always a go-getter, they say.

Chapter 4

"Speak to me Lord
For your child is here listening
Speak to me Lord
For your child is here waiting on You
Unveil my eyes let me see—see You
Unveil my heart let me know—know
You"

Speak to Me by Rebecca St. James

CATHERINE

I am sitting quietly, alone in my room. It looks like not long after I got sick. I remember longing for God in those moments. I fidget and breathe deeply. It takes me a while to settle my thoughts. When I finally find the quiet inside me, I begin. Sitting comfortably, I open my bible and thumb through for the right page. I stop on Psalm 6. I take a deep breath and begin.

"Lord, don't be angry and rebuke me!" I read tenderly. "Don't punish me in your anger! I am worn out, O Lord; have pity on me! Give me strength; I am completely exhausted and my whole being is deeply troubled. How long, O Lord, will you wait to help me?"

I turn to Jesus, waiting for Him to speak, but He sits beside me as I pray. He smiles at me lovingly and whispers in my ear. "Strength," I write in my journal.

'*My life*', I think, '*how does this speak to my life?*' I start again, "Lord, don't be angry and rebuke me!" I read more fervently. "Don't punish me in your anger! I am worn out, O Lord; have pity on me! Give me strength; I am completely exhausted and my whole being is deeply troubled. How long, O Lord, will you wait to help me?"

Again, He whispers in my ear, this time wrapping an arm around my shoulder as well.

I begin to write again. "I have to be strong… but… but what does that mean? How can I be strong now… now that I'm dying?" I see the words appearing on the page in my journal.

What am I called to change? What challenges do I need to overcome? How is God calling me? One last time I begin again, "Lord, don't be angry and rebuke me!" I read intently. "Don't punish me in your anger! I am worn out, O Lord; have pity on me! Give me strength; I am completely exhausted and my whole being is deeply troubled. How long, O Lord, will you wait to help me?"

Jesus points to the book and is whispering in my ear again. He is excited and hugs me.

Suddenly, I am alone in the cathedral. I look to the altar and ambo at the front of the church, but I only see the light beaming through the windows, catching the dust floating through the air. I begin walking among the pews looking up and down them. My heart jumps to my throat, maybe He... '*I'm being silly,*' I think. He probably has other... obligations; being the Son of God and all.

"I'm always with you," He says from a little side chapel to my right. He is kneeling, praying. I let out a sigh of relief as He rises to His feet and continues, "I'm with every one of God's children." I look at Him confused, so He continues, "All things are possible, through Me, remember."

He returns to His spot praying. I kneel beside Him dutifully.

BRICE

I am looking at myself as a child. I am in my room alone. I pick up a book and thumb through it, then put it down again. I slump onto my bed. My face is downcast. I look out the window and see the sun shining through a gap in the clouds. I am surprised when Jesus goes and sits next to me on my bed. He puts an arm around my shoulder, and I sigh deeply.

"God... if you're really out there..." I begin. I look out my bedroom window and see the same tree I've seen for years, but I notice something else for the first time. Behind the tree is a tall white church steeple.

We are back inside the chapel. I look beside me, but I appear to be all alone. My heart sinks, but then I notice a beam of light at the front of the chapel. Jesus is kneeling where the light hits the floor. I walk over to Him and kneel beside Him

50

quietly. I stay there as long as I can before exhaustion overwhelms me.

I awake crumpled on the floor. I sigh in disappointment with myself.

"No need for that," He says kindly. "We have things to do."

I am outside my parents' house. I am nervous as I enter. It's just dinner, I tell myself.

No one is in the front room when I enter. I leave my jacket in the closet and head to the kitchen. I might as well see if I can help.

From the look of it, Mom is putting the finishing touches on the meal.

"Can I take things to the table?" I offer.

"Oh, hi Brice, yeah," she says absent-mindedly. "It's just the three of us though." She sighs.

One less person for me to offend, I guess.

After bustling back and forth a few times, my dad, my mom, and myself are seated around the table. I pause, ready to pray, but they begin to eat. I silently say one before I start.

"How's school?" my dad asks, clearly distracted.

"Fine," I respond.

"Don't forget we have a luncheon after church Sunday—no you can't get out of going to church with me again," my mom says.

Here we go.

"About that, I'm"—I clear my throat to build up my confidence—"I'm not going, I want to go to a different church."

She drops her fork and looks up at me. "Where?" she asks, directly and sternly. "What's wrong with Park Avenue Christian? It's where *we* as a family go."

"I don't fit in, I just want to try—"

"You could fit in, if you try!" She shoves her chair back and storms out of the room.

My dad glares at me over the frames of his glasses and says, "Don't upset your mother like that. Just go with her and on your own time you can do whatever you want."

"No," I say quietly, "it's not"—I stop when I see my dad's face. I put my fork down and go to get my jacket. I hang my head as I start to put one arm in my sleeve.

"I don't know where I went wrong with you," my mom says snidely from down the hall.

I stiffen, but I am firm in my resolve. This is what's right for me, why can't she see that? I love that she has her place and her community. Now I've found mine.

"I don't expect you to go, but"—I clear my throat—"I will be baptized in the Church of Jesus Christ of Latter Day Saints at the end of the month."

"You won't go with me because you're going to… to *that* church?" she asks with disdain.

I hear her begin to cry and yell, but I simply walk out the front door. The last thing I hear is her saying, "They're not even Christian! Not really."

I'm at the chapel, but it's full of people. I swell with pride as I recognize what day it is. It is the day I was baptized. I barely see or hear anything that is actually happening as I am so overcome with jubilation. And to think now I get to experience this momentous occasion with my Lord. My eyes brim over with tears of joy.

Jesus smiles. It is good to have him proud of me for once.

"Not only once, but every day, my child." He hugs me. Things couldn't be better.

It is good to celebrate finding the light. There is a reception after the baptism and we are all overjoyed. The elation of this time fills me even now, watching it from the outside. Until a moment of sadness sets in; it is a moment my family did not attend, did not revel in, did not understand. I had turned my back on their church and therefore in their eyes, it must be a mistake. I found what spoke to me, but it caused deep division in my life. If only they would just understand this is what was right for me! I hate that such a happy time is also so bittersweet, but I won't let it ruin my joy.

The Johnsons, a couple around my parents' age, beam at me as if I were their own son. As I look around, I see I don't need them; this is my family. I have a family in this place, with these people. There is still an emptiness inside though.

I jump to a memory a few months later. It is the Sunday before Christmas, and it will be my first Christmas alone. My parents and I have not spoken for months. After my baptism, my mom cried, and not joyful tears, so I have not returned to their house. At least, not yet. I cannot help but feel less holiday cheer and very lonely. I take a seat in the back. I am glad that I am here, where I belong, but I don't want to draw attention to my solitude. I swallow my sadness and try to smile. The coming of our Lord, it is a joyous time!

"Hello, Brice!" Mrs. Johnson says, smiling. "Merry Christmas! Are you excited for some family time?"

"Actually…" But I avoid eye contact rather than finish my thought.

She drops to the pew next to me with a knowing glance and gives me a squeeze around my shoulders.

"But you can't spend Christmas alone!"

I look up just enough to see the couple exchange knowing glances, before Mr. Johnson chimes in, "Join us for our family dinner on Christmas. No, no we insist!" He waves away my feeble interjection.

"And don't worry about bringing anything," Mrs. Johnson says. "Just come on over. We're all family in a way; just spend it with some extended members," she adds warmly.

My loneliness is all but evaporated. I try to think of some kindness I can do for the couple in return. At least she's right. I have family here.

We are back at the empty chapel and I feel an emptiness inside. This place had just been filled with so many people who touched my life, but now… now it is empty, hallow.

I see Jesus sitting in a pew with His head bowed, hands folded in prayer. I sit next to Him and follow suit, happy I am not completely alone.

CATHERINE

I am following my mom into the basilica, ducking behind her skirt as it flows around her swift legs. She sits with some women and pulls out the beads I so desperately want to play with: they are so pretty and sparkly. She won't let me touch them usually, but when we come here, she gives me my own strand. I have to be good and follow along to get them though. I try to remember how to start when the women begin, "In the name of the Father and the Son and the Holy Spirit. I believe in God, the Father almighty, creator of heaven and earth. I believe in Jesus Christ, his only Son, our Lord, who was conceived by the Holy Spirit and born of the Virgin Mary…."

I fidget in my seat and my mom places a hand on my lap reminding me to be still.

The next part begins and I try to follow my mom's lead about which bead to hold. "Our Father…" they begin. Proud at how well I know this prayer I pipe up along with the women, drawing a smile from one woman across the circle of chairs.

I look down in time to see my mom change beads and quickly follow. "The first Sorrowful Mystery, The Agony in the Garden. Hail Mary, full of grace…"

I try to follow, but as they repeat the prayers and move the beads and occasionally announce another 'mystery,' I struggle to keep my eyes from wandering.

I look up at the stained-glass window of a dove and smile. '*What a pretty bird,*' I think.

The older me turns to Jesus, but He isn't standing beside me. That's when I see Him sitting with my child-self, smiling and laughing. He's playing with the dust in the sunlight above me and the child smiles and stares in wonder at how the particles dance above her. It's touching to see that He was there even then. He has always been there for me, even if I did turn away from Him for a while.

BRICE

Again, I startle awake. This time, I'm laying down in a pew. Jesus is sitting by my feet. He pats my leg. "Rest enough?"

I jump to a seated position, a little too fast, and swoon. '*Odd,*' I think, but I take a deep breath and simply say, "Yes."

I smile as I see my family again, gathering around for their evening prayer. It is touching to join them again.

I gasp as I see a younger version of myself join them right next to where I am standing, "That's—so that's me. So, this is a memory of the past?"

"No, we're here, and they're here and it's the present," Jesus says, thoroughly confusing me. I soften when I see the prayer begin.

"Dear Heavenly Father..." the younger version of myself begins. I look at my wife and am drawn over to her. I miss her and wonder when she will join me as I reach out to touch her hair.

56

I draw my hand back solemnly. That was a selfish wish, I think to myself. Of course, I want her to live a long and happy life. It's just, I miss her so.

Suddenly I'm back in the chapel.

I notice Jesus by the baptismal font as I scan the room for Him. I walk up to Him but am silent. His fingers gently skim the surface of the water. Ripples spread and collide in endless patterns. There is peace at that moment. The light is shining brightly down on Him through a high window, creating a heavenly aura around Him.

'This is my beloved son,' I think to try to remember the rest of the verse.

Chapter 5

"They gave our Master a crown of thorns, why do we hope for a crown of roses?"

Martin Luther

CATHERINE

Back at the church, it is peaceful, though it is increasingly messy. Things are falling off the walls; pieces of drywall and even bricks are scattered about everywhere. I find a spot where a pew is mostly intact and lay on my side, curling my feet up. Jesus comes and sits next to me. It is a comfort knowing He is watching while I rest. I drift off as He gently strokes my hair.

I am calm and collected when I wake. I again start to notice the demons lurking in dark shadows, but I don't want to deal with that now.

"That is the problem with demons. Or why they become a problem," Jesus says.

"What?"

"That you don't want to 'deal with them.'"

I start to wonder what my demons really are, but it is so confusing at times like this. I want something that makes sense.

A sound somewhere between a purr and a growl comes from so close by it makes me jump. I'm a little afraid to look around for the source of the noise, but I don't want a surprise attack either. I look in every direction except where I now realize it is. It is right next to me, on my left. It—it's cuddled up to me! The demon is acting like a pet or something. Is this what taming your demons means?

"No, you still have work to do. Don't be fooled by your perception of things."

"So don't trust it."

"I didn't say that."

"I'm sorry, but I need to understand. What is it? What am I supposed to do with it? What"—I look down on my arm and there are scratches. The damn thing scratched me!

"It is a part of you, and you need to heal it too."

I think I see a shadow move at that last word. These can't really be a part of me.

"But they are," He says.

I'm going to have to be more careful about what I'm thinking—

"That's not really the point. What you call purgatory isn't what you think it is. It's a chance to finally become everything you are always intended to be, to be in full, uninhibited, vulnerable, intimate communion with God and each other. Like in the garden."

"So, Eden is a real place?"

"It's as real as you need it to be. There was a time when everything was in communion with each other and there was a time that was broken. Truth isn't about historic records; it's about so much more than that. Truth is about what is in your heart. The rest is just details." He let me think quietly for a moment before continuing, "Are you ready to begin?"

"I guess so," I respond.

We are in another memory with Theodore.

"Can't I ever be rid of him?" I say under my breath, but I knew Jesus would hear it even if I didn't actually say it out loud.

Theodore leans in to whisper in my ear. I turn away from the scene, disgusted.

"I can't face this," I snap. "I wasn't in a good place. I mean clearly." I vaguely gesture to my younger self. "I was young and stupid."

"Don't be so hard on yourself," Jesus says kindly. "That isn't what this is about."

"So what? I need to start making up for—atoning for my stupidity?"

"I didn't say you needed to atone for this." He walks closer and gently takes my hand.

He holds out his hands and they are now covered in blood.

I gasp.

"I don't understand. What's—Why..." I can't even finish my questions through my tears.

"Your pain is my pain." His voice cracks a little as he says, "We'll walk this journey of healing together."

My pride disappears as I simply say, "Okay."

Tears stream down Jesus' cheeks.

"I—"

He smiles through the streaks.

"I'm sorry about that outburst. I just—I didn't mean to hurt *you*."

"People rarely do."

I sigh. "So anger isn't working, what do I need to do?"

"Face it. Heal from it."

"I know." His hands have stopped bleeding. Is this what I'm supposed to be doing? Is it working? At least I know Theodore will suffer for what he did to me.

"Focus on you. I'll worry about him." Jesus wraps an arm around me. "Right here."

I tuck my chin down and through my blur of tears, I notice my tunic looks a bit cleaner. I think it is working.

"Exactly."

"That's unnerving, you know."

"I know, but what do you expect from the *All-Knowing*."

"How about some respectful boundaries."

A huge grin spreads across his face. "Now we're talking. About time you learn to set better boundaries."

"Wait, what? You want me to be in communion with you, but we start with boundaries?"

"Yes." He takes a deep breath before continuing. "Being in communion doesn't mean you lose you."

"Oh." I have no idea what he means.

"A drop of water is not lost in the ocean."

"So, you're a Buddhist, not a Christian? 'Cuz that's what you just sounded like."

"Actually, technically I'm neither. I am Jewish." We both laugh.

"Seriously, think about a drop of water, does it stop being water in the ocean?"

I can see a vast expanse of water now as he describes his metaphor.

"I... I don't think so." My brain hurts trying to remember what little I learned about science. Does anything cause water to stop being water? Not in the ocean, right? I'm not a scientist, so how should I know?

He chuckles. "I revel in all my Father's creation. Science could have taught you a lot more about it. And me." He draws in a long breath before continuing. "No, a drop of water doesn't stop being water in the ocean. They're all hydrogen and oxygen and while they mix and immerse themselves in each other, they are still each hydrogen and oxygen. There are things that can divide the elements and add other elements, but that's not what I'm talking about now."

"So I'm supposed to be close to others, but not lose myself," I say slowly. I can see how I've been getting all my relationships wrong all along.

"Now you are starting to understand intimacy."

BRICE

As I look around the halls of my junior high, I am filled with dread, but if we have to go through every little pain from my life, we might as well start here. I can see the scrawny, timid, younger version of myself by my old locker. I see him coming and even now I shrink away. I see something out of the corner of my eye that distracts me though. Is something crawling on the wall? That isn't right, there isn't anything in the school except for people. I suddenly feel my heart pounding in my throat. Is this my memory or a horror movie? What if I don't move on to a better place?

I can see my bully walks by me and sort of shoves me, but I manage to walk away relatively unscathed. I know moments like that hurt, but I didn't think I would have to work through them like this.

I turn to Jesus. "It was nothing," I say. "I mean I don't have the time to go through every little memory that hurt."

Jesus smiles. "Okay, let's move on then," is all He says.

CATHERINE

"Catherine," says a soft voice, rousing me.

I'm sitting in front of a statue quietly. I didn't even realize I had spaced out. "This is nice here," I respond.

"You can stay here if you like," He says sadly.

"I can?"

"Yes."

"Jennifer and other people can join me?"

"No, not until you heal."

I sigh. "No, I can't stay. What's next?"

We're in another memory or whatever these are. We're at the park. I remember that day.

"Really? Do I have to make up with her? I barely even snapped at her."

Jesus just smiles. "You need to heal."

"Ugh. Okay, what do I have to do this time?"

He shrugged. "It's your life—your pain. You tell me."

"I was exhausted. Overworked, underpaid, I had my daughter to take care of and…"

"And?"

"No one to take care of me. It got better—but not until after it got worse. A lot worse."

"And?"

The scene is playing out as we speak. Gracie asking for help, the lady barging in, I snap at her and in the end, we leave.

Tears welled in my eyes. I didn't want to say it, but clearly, I had to.

"That was right after Jennifer died. I lost my sister and I"—my voice broke. My heart is breaking all over again. "I hadn't told Gracie yet that she lost her aunt, I—I just wanted one more carefree day at the park. I always admired how proud Gracie was when she did things by herself. She would just brim over with delight. I needed that joy at that moment."

"It's the little things that get us through the tough times."

Tears well in my eyes and spill onto my cheeks. "I just wanted to be left alone."

"Really? Because it looks to me like you could have used a friend," He says as the younger me walks away with my daughter.

"Gracie, I need to talk to you about Aunt Jennifer." *'How can I talk to my daughter about the death of her beloved aunt? How can I tell her Jennifer died of anorexia?'*

We are back at the church and I can't believe my eyes.

Jesus is standing before me with His crown of thorns digging into His head and dripping blood all around His face. I feel relief that the blood all seems to be around His face and not—but I suppose that will come also if this has.

"Yes, my child, I am crucified every day in one way or another."

"I"—tears fill my eyes as my voice cracks. This is too much to see. I'm not even the one going through it, but I can't witness this.

"I'm here. You are not alone in your pain."

"Is—is that why—"

"Yes."

I collapse in a heap on the pew. My sobbing continues until it feels like there are no more tears in the universe, let alone in me.

We are sitting on the floor. More pews have toppled to one side or the other. I must be a real wreck to have my sin and pain cause this much damage. '*Or maybe I'm this damaged*?' I think somberly.

"We all are," Jesus says.

"What?"

"We all are this damaged." Jesus waves His hand around. "In our own way." His brow, all along His head; He is bleeding. The crimson drops are streaming down His face and through His hair. He is sitting next to me as we lean against the side of a broken pew.

"How do we fix all this?"

"One board, one nail at a time."

I smile. "You are a carpenter after all."

BRICE

I'm at work now. It's when I was a pharmacy tech. I was much happier even though my dad looked down on it. If I became a pharmacist, that's a different story, but a technician? "Where's the pride in being someone's assistant?" I can still hear my dad say to me.

Still, I was happy. I can read my own thoughts as I watch the scene unfold. Home could have been better. Sophie and I have been trying for several months now and still no sign of a baby. *'How could you do this, God? I'm doing everything right, aren't I? We just want to bring more life and love to the world.'*

I am snapped out of my thoughts by a woman coming to the pharmacy counter with a crumpled prescription paper. She seems edgy; is she trying to get something to sell? I've learned to stay on guard with some people.

"Can I help you?" I say.

"Yeah I need this." She turns red.

I look at the script and hand it back. I can't believe some people. "I can't fill this."

Then there are all the women out there who just take it for granted, throw a life away. Haven't they heard of adoption? Anything is better than abortion.

"I… but, my doctor…" she mumbles.

"You have other options you know," I say. If only I could convince her. If only my wife was in her position…

"I… look this is between me and my doctor. He wrote me a prescription, so fill it!" she snaps.

"It's murder," is all I can say in response, so I walk away as tears fill my eyes. Someone else can deal with that. "If only, if only," I say to myself as I walk away. "We'd love that child."

Back at the church, relief washes over me. "Finally something in my life I got right!" I exclaim.

Jesus' sorrow quickly turns. "What makes you think that?" He snaps.

"I… uh… the unborn baby… You want me to protect life, especially such an innocent life. That baby didn't do anything to deserve to be killed!" I can't believe this.

Jesus sighs. "She miscarried. The *medication* was to prevent sepsis after a miscarriage."

I sit down without even noticing the stuffing on the seat. "I… didn't…" I choke out between gasps.

"'For I tell you, unless your righteousness exceeds that of the scribes and Pharisees, you will never enter the kingdom of heaven.'"

"Matthew 5:20," I say almost automatically. I can't believe what I'm hearing. Am I no greater than a Pharisee? This can't be happening.

"So, I'm a Pharisee?" I sigh. "I was just trying to do what was right."

"So were they."

Shock washes over me. How awful. And how awful I was to her!

"Exactly," Jesus replies to my thought.

Green eyes are glowing to my left.

"Not you again," I say. "I guess I have to deal with you sometime." I swing a swift kick at it as it hisses back at me.

"That's right, get out of here!" I yell as it retreats away.

"You'll never get rid of them that way," Jesus remarks.

I shake my head and turn my attention to a pile of dust nearby.

Left alone without the distraction of the demons, my mind wanders back to my last memory. I can't bear what just happened. There has to be something else I can focus on rather than that woman, that abor—that mis—that baby.

"So where's our next stop on the tour of my life?" I ask, still eyeing the demon across the aisle. This place is… it's not what it used to be. I can't wait to get away from here.

"Some things need to be torn down to be rebuilt."

"Okay, I guess," I mumble.

"Are you sure you don't want to rest first?"

"No, I'm sure. I'm more than ready to get out of here."

Some larger dog-like demons with unnerving eyes have come out of the shadows, far more menacing than the one I scared away. What are they doing here?

"Really, I'm ready. What's next?"

I am in my memory now and… I steel myself as recognition sets in. My mom and my brother are ahead of me, barely noticing me dragging along behind them. We are almost home. A tear streams down my cheek as I think about what the unsuspecting younger me will face behind that door. I suck in a slow breath and will the tears back. Men don't cry, after all.

"I weep," Jesus says gently. Tears are streaming down his cheeks as blood drips from his fingertips and this time from his forehead and side. The sight of my Savior so broken and bleeding opens a wellspring inside of me. He opens his arms and I accept his embrace, mixing my tears with his and his blood. He holds me as I begin to sob.

When I open my eyes, we are back at the chapel and Jesus is talking to someone quietly. I walk to the spot and am taken aback when I see my demons around Him, among the dust and debris.

"What?" I gasp.

"I was telling them about my own demons. It comforts them."

I open and close my mouth trying to think of a response.

"Yes, I had demons, too, though on a different scale," He says with a smile. "Why do you think it took me 40 days? For someone who's perfect?" He winks at me.

Chapter 6

"You were as I
Tempted and trialed
Human
The word became flesh
Bore my sin and death
Now you're risen

Everything I once held dear
I count it all as loss

Lead me to the cross
Where Your love poured out
Bring me to my knees
Lord I lay me down
Rid me of myself
I belong to You
Lead me, lead me to the cross"

Lead Me to the Cross by Hillsong
United

CATHERINE

We are in my memory now and... my heart
sinks. It's when I met Theodore.

"I guess I have to face this eventually," I sigh. "I know I was wrong to ever let him in my life." My expression hardens.

"That is not what this is about. He wasn't good for you, but you are not the one to blame."

"So I'm the victim? I hate that word. If I had just been smarter, seen the signs, been stronger... strong enough to stand up to him. Strong enough to walk away sooner..." Tears stream down my cheeks as I watch the scene play out in front of me. I am sitting outside a little café, reading a book, and pretending not to notice anyone around me. He strolls up to me, all flirty and confident. I always wanted to be that confident. We talk and laugh. He is not lude or suggestive, but touches my arm, tilts his head to one side. The way he smiles makes his intentions quite clear.

"Can I have your number?" I hear him say.

No, I want to scream. It's all fake, don't do it, don't fall for it this time!

"Okay," is all I can squeak out as a reply.

"So this is my cross." I turn away from the scene.

"No child, your cross is what you chose to bear."

"So I didn't have one?" I say in shock.

"You need to look at it a little differently."

I nod, but I have no idea what He is talking about. Your cross is your burden. This sure feels like a heavy burden.

"Catherine, your cross is more complicated than that." He pauses. "And at once simpler. It's not how or why or what it is. Your cross is that you care so much; some would say too much. You are willing to feel hurt with others."

"Oh," I say. That wasn't what I was expecting.

BRICE

A very different scene flashes into view. My wife, children, and I are walking through a health fair. It has some good information for all of us and is a learning experience for the kids. Plus, it is something to do on a lazy afternoon off work and school.

We pass a booth for blood donations and I stop and sign up. Sophie is too squeamish about the needles but encourages me. Besides, someone has to wrangle three rambunctious kids while I do it. A little idle chat and I am all hooked up and the blood is pumping. It is a strange sensation, like the life being drained out of me, but only a little. It is definitely a tiring process, yet I know the benefit that comes from giving it to others. I register to be an organ donor also; every little bit helps.

They offer me a magazine, but I decide to take this time in quiet reflection; to be grateful for all God has given me. I look over at my wife and children and smile. I see Peia try to make a break for it, but the ever vigilant Jax nabs her after four steps. She struggles so he tickles her playfully. Devin takes advantage of the distraction to steal a lingering hug from Sophie. It is at least two full minutes before Peia spots Devin in Sophie's lap and starts to cry. Pouting, Devin relinquishes Sophie's lap only to get playfully tackled by Jax. Jax is always there for

Devin, too. I look at the four of them and smile. Life couldn't be better.

We wrap up at the blood drive and move on around the health fair. We stop and read fliers here, the kids get to play a game there. It all starts to blur into a lazy afternoon and my attention to the memory wanes.

"I have to say, I'm not really sure what is so important," I say as I turn to Jesus and continue, "I mean of course my family is the most important part of my life, but—but any number of memories would show that and"—I let out a deep sigh. I'm not sure I should say this, but I'm going to anyway. "And You've made your point." There, I challenged someone I have no authority to challenge, but it's out there.

"Have I?" is all Jesus says and points to a booth in the middle of an aisle we are walking down. Not many people are stopping, and few out of those who do stop actually sign up.

Curious, I walk closer. What am I missing?

I reach the booth and see it is another donor drive, but a very different one. It is to get people to sign up to be a bone marrow donor. There are a few pictures and statistics.

"Most bone marrow donors are family members. While this is important, not everyone has a compatible family member to do so," I read out loud. Is this what I missed? To my horror, Sophie and I glance at the booth and keep walking. Peia is getting antsy, so it's time to get the family home.

"But—but I was an organ donor," I stammer, "I— I thought… It was supposed to do the same sort of thing, but—I guess the accident—there wasn't much to donate after that."

"No, there wasn't."

"So…" My hands drop to my side, defeated. "I should have given more," I mumble.

Jesus reaches a hand down to take mine. "It's never about what you *should* have done." He smiles and looks deeply into my eyes. "Only what you need to heal. This needs to be healed. Yes, you could have helped someone if you signed up today and that hurt her—and you in the process, but it is simply another thing to face and let go of. Let go, child."

CATHERINE

We're back at the empty church. Dust and dirt are everywhere, drifting off the rafters, in small piles on broken pews and the window ledges. There are now large cobwebs in the corners.

A shadow over my head draws my focus up. Something flies to a rafter, but as soon as it lights on the beam, a crash booms through the space. The beam's left side crashes through the pews across the aisle from me. The right side of the beam remains mostly connected to the roof, leaving the beam swinging like a giant battering ram. The demon hovers where the beam was, still shocked by its sudden disappearance. As it pauses there flapping, I catch a better view of the creature. It has bat-like wings, but otherwise, it seems more cat-like; fluffy and plump. A well-fed cat for sure. The eyes are a piercing golden color with multiple eyelids blinking across as well as down. It looks at me as it settles cautiously on the next rafter. It surveys the room with a lofty glance. What, does it think it owns the place?

"Ugh," I sigh, "When is this place going to get cleaned up?"

"When we start cleaning it."

"Wait, that's *my* job?"

"It's our project. Together. We need to do a little more work on your life first, then we can really get to work rebuilding. Once you get the hang of things."

"I'm not sure what to do," I say as I run my finger across a crack in a nearby pew.

"I'm a carpenter, remember."

BRICE

I sit on a mostly intact chair and sulk. Did I bring Christ's love to the world? I thought I did. I was so sure of it, but now... A rather large demon jumps out of a shadow, startling me. It looked meaner than the other ones I've seen. I look at it and back at Jesus. I look back and forth between the two again and then again before it dawns on me. "That's—that's my hate, that demon. Isn't it?"

"Yes. It's your wrath."

I take a deep breath, "Okay, I'm ready to face it." I had steel in my veins, so was my resolve. I can face anything.

"That still isn't what's helpful. Try softening up a bit," Jesus says.

"Be soft? With evil?"

"How many times do I need to tell you it's a part of you?"

I stand baffled. I am still not sure what I am supposed to do with these things?

Jesus is leaning against a pew with a net in His hands. An actual fishing net. I am so confused.

I don't know if I've seen a net in real life. I examine the pattern woven throughout the net. It is mesmerizing and intricate. Jesus appears to be mending a spot.

"It is good to make things with my own hands," He says, then adds, "reminds me I'm alive." His dark eyes glisten.

I look over His shoulder at a painting of Jesus by the seashore calling to the fishermen in a boat.

"Now, where were we?" He asks.

Chapter 7

"What if I lose my step
And I make fools of us all?
Will the love continue
When my walk becomes a crawl?
What if I stumble
And what if I fall?"

What If I Stumble? by DC Talk

CATHERINE

We're in my junior high and I am walking with my friends and boyfriend. I definitely have things to make up for here. Of course I was a snobby teenager. Who wasn't?

Jesus clears his throat.

"Actually, I seem to recall you running away from your parents and being a little mouthy to your mom," I say.

He laughs. "I wasn't a teenager yet, but good to know you have a *thorough* understanding of the Bible."

My group of friends pass another kid and give a scoff, but keep walking. He looks kinda sad—and lonely, I realize. How many people did I ignore in my self-absorbed teen angst? Do I have to make it up to all of them?

"No, I said you have to heal your relationships with them. That's not exactly the same as 'making it up to them.' People can heal without words and without face to face interactions. You are already starting to show compassion for others; they will know that here. You need to heal inside yourself."

"But some people I will have to face."

"Yes, the people you need to heal with the most." When He sees the dread on my face, he adds, "But not until you're ready."

"All these people I hurt by what I said and did," I sulk.

"Just everyone you need to heal your relationship with; actually, some are people you didn't talk to when you had the chance."

I'm in a different memory now, though still in high school. This time we're at a stupid peer conflict resolution class.

"Maybe that's part of the problem," Jesus leans into me and says.

I blush and fluster trying to find a response.

"Mr. Jones," the younger me pipes up. "I think I get it now," I say sweetly. "We need to be more compassionate. Everyone has problems and we're all just trying to get through." I blink away a crocodile tear. I was always good at telling people what they wanted to hear.

"Exactly, Catherine," the teacher says. "You've really come a long way."

"Okay, I admit it. I was being fake. Totally lying. I just wanted the stupid thing over. But my bullying wasn't even *that* bad."

Jesus looks at me with raised eyebrows, not saying a word, but I get the message.

"Okay, so it was," I sulk. "I was pretty awful at times. I have a lot to be ashamed of."

"You have some things to feel guilty about. Shame isn't useful," Jesus corrects.

I turn to face Him. "What's the difference?"

"Guilt tells you you're doing something wrong and you need to knock it off. You feel guilty when you hurt someone. It also shows you care. This is a lot harder when there aren't any guilty feelings," He raises one eyebrow and smirks a little. "Back to the point, it's a burden, but it's an easy fix; change your behavior. Turn to me, return to loving, even small efforts show."

"So, what's shame then?"

"Shame isn't about what you do. People feel shame about who they are. And sometimes about what's happened to you." He gives me a side glance that I avoid by looking down intently at my fingernails.

He wraps His arm around my shoulder in a warm embrace. "That isn't why we're here. This is." He points and I look up again.

The younger me goes out in the hall with my friends as class ends. They look at me and snicker as a nerdy girl walks by.

"Hey, wait up," I call to her and leave my friends behind, still snickering.

"Sorry—ahem—sorry about my friends," I tell her.

"It's okay," she says shyly. "I'm used to it. I'll be alright."

"Where do you get your hair done?" I run my fingers through her long hair flowing over her shoulders.

She looks deeply into her locker, embarrassed. "My mom just trims it at home," she replies.

"No one could tell," I say, mocking surprise.

She stiffens, catching my tone. She finishes grabbing what she needs from her locker. "Well, off to class," she says through gritted teeth.

"What's the hurry?" I say grabbing her shoulder. My friends are behind me, now laughing.

"Look," I add, quickly getting to the point, "just quit the team already. It's not like you're any good."

Sophie looks down. "I—I can't," she stammers, "my mom won't let me. Says I need the experience for college applications and—and to make friends."

I laugh. "Yeah, lot of good that's doing."

I slam her locker door shut on her, making her jump. "Just quit."

I walk away with my friends laughing, but inside I can only think about my locked bedroom door that is waiting for me at home. The door that only locks when we lose.

"I shouldn't have picked on her, I know," the older me says and turns away. My shoulders sag. Guilt is a heavy burden.

BRICE

Bryan comes up behind me, grabbing my shoulders from behind, laughing as I flinch. He walks around to his seat. As usual, no one cares that he is late. He takes the bread roll off my plate. Not like it was the one decent part of the meal. My mom shoots me a 'just drop it' look as she hands me another.

"Could you go get me a pop out of the garage?" Mom asks.

"Sure," I say, and stand. As I reach the door, Bryan interjects, "Me too."

"You do it," I spit back.

"You're already there," Mom says.

I grab two and put them on the table. When I sit, I sink lower in my seat, but I turn to my dad and quietly say, "I'm going over to Billy's after dinner to work on some homework."

Without looking up from his plate, he replies, "You can do homework here. You need to focus more; fewer distractions." He waves a hand at the last word.

"It's meant to be completed with a friend. Part of the grade is working together or whatever."

"You'll fail then," Bryan laughs, "Who would want to be your friend?"

I fight back tears every time he jabs at me this way, which is almost daily, but I can't let him have the satisfaction of seeing me cry.

"Couldn't it be done sooner?" My dad sighs. "I wish you would stop waiting until the last minute for everything." He finally looks up. "Fine, do what you need to, then come right home! By nine!"

I finish my plate and slink over to the sink to put my dishes away. I can't wait to get away from here, even if it was for a lie, I don't feel guilty. It's not like I'm sneaking off to drink or meet a girl. I just can't wait to be anywhere else.

I realize we're back at the church, but it is even more of mess.

"I can't believe I have to make up for that lie!" I say to Jesus.

He looks back at me with one eyebrow raised, "I never said you had to 'make up for' anything. This is a place of healing."

The memory changes around me. I don't recognize where I am. I think I'm in front of another church. Great, I am not good enough at converting them, or I'm in the wrong one... No, that can't be it.

"Do you know why we're here?"

"I'm not sure. Maybe I don't do enough here."

"No, do you know why you aren't in heaven yet?"

"Because... because I'm not perfect. I mean, no one is."

"I am."

Show off. I couldn't help the reactive thought popping in my mind. My face burns with shame. Just move on. "So, what do I need to do? You know do I... I mean I have accepted you. I... I thought that was it. I've lived a pretty good life. I didn't kill anyone or do anything *that* bad."

"It is true you are a good man. You always have been a good person. You have accepted me into your life. And yet there is still division from you and others. You have not accepted *them* into your heart." He nods to a group of people sitting in the grass in front of the church preparing for a summer bible camp or something.

I pondered his words for a while. What haven't I accepted about others? Really, am I not being a good enough person?

"What you call heaven is... it's nothing you can imagine, but it's full communion with me and everyone else. It's letting go of everything you've done and everything that's been done to you."

"We've already established I don't do much—"

"Exactly. It's not always what you do to hurt someone, but what you don't do that hurts them."

"So, I am supposed to know every time I needed to do something for someone?"

"This isn't about what you are 'supposed' to do. It's about what you need to do now to move on to full communion. One hurt at a time. One person at a time."

"So how did I hurt them?" I nod to the group.

"I never said you did."

Then why did you bring me here?" I scream. I take a breath. I don't mean to yell. It doesn't make sense to me. We have things to talk about or whatever, so why waste time? Let's move on, get things rolling. We don't have all eternity. I'd like to spend some of it somewhere pleasant. I'd really like to move on to seeing my Peia again.

CATHERINE

We're on the street now. It's late, or early. Looks like dawn may break soon. I don't see myself or anyone familiar yet. I want to ask why we're here, but I never seem to like the answers to my questions, so I wait. I am sure it will become clear. Eventually.

Jesus smiles and rubs his arms in the cold. Wait—he gets cold?

"I am human." He lifts one eyebrow and continues, "It's always coldest just before the dawn." He points down the street. Finally, I see myself walking, and—my heart sinks. I know what night—or morning, this is now.

The younger me is stumbling a little, though I am not drunk. He couldn't use that excuse against me, not that I would have deserved it if I had been drinking.

I'm shivering. I left my jacket when I ran out of his place.

"Need to borrow a coat?" a man asks. I don't remember him. I had a lot on my mind.

"No thank you," I say, and look down.

"You ok?" he says.

"I'm fine," I lie, and keep walking.

"Okay, just asking," he mumbles as I turn the corner. He looks concerned for me but continues on his way since I am long gone.

"I know there's some big insight I'm supposed to have right now, but—I don't get it. Why here?"

"We'll get to the really tough part of that night, but right now we're easing into some things." Jesus looks deeply into my eyes with His penetrating stare. "You needed help, but weren't willing to receive it," He says bluntly.

At least He laid it right out there.

"I"—tears start to stream down my cheeks—"I didn't think he'd believe me. Or he'd say I deserved it, so—so I just wanted to get away. I couldn't stand to be around anyone, even myself."

"He only offered you a coat and his concern, and you shunned it when you needed it. 'When you do it to the least of my brothers' isn't just about giving. It's also about receiving. It's about building relationship. Love exists in the space between two people."

"God is love," I whisper.

"Yes. People see Love as a noun or even a verb, but it's—I'm—both—and neither."

"Love exists in the space between people," I repeat, pondering this statement. "I never thought about it that way."

"People rarely do."

"But—you said I needed better boundaries. Before, you said—"

He smiles. "I remember. Boundaries sometimes need to be firmer and sometimes need to be put down. You are your own person, don't lose yourself, but let people in, let love exist between you. Catherine, with you it's all or nothing."

"I—" This was a lot more to take in that I thought.

"That's enough from this night for now. Let's rest before we move on." He puts his arm around my shoulder.

"Sounds good," I mumble.

We're at the church again. I push through a pile of broken wood and cushion stuffing, but I don't see Him. I turn to my left, but all I see are broken pews and scattered debris. I turn to my right and walk between some pews, but I can't find Him.

I see something in the main aisle, so I start to sprint. Sure enough, He is there, but He is on one knee looking down in exhaustion. I run over to help Him up.

"I'm okay," He says weakly.

I don't believe Him, but I won't argue.

He rises to His feet and already the color is returning to His face. He smiles and says, "What's next?" As if I was controlling all this memory jumping.

BRICE

"You'll see her again soon."

I steel myself. Okay, I can do whatever is asked of me if it means I will see my beloved daughter again.

"Okay, so why am I here? Like here in front of this church. I don't even remember which one it is. Saint something of something. Is it the Catholic one?" Great, *they* are right?

"It's not about being right or wrong. All religions have something of truth in them and... well, all are developed by humans and therefore are fallible. There is no right way. And no wrong one really. Only me and as long as you find deeper communion with God and each other."

"God is love."

He smiles. "Exactly what I was just thinking."

I think for a while. I can't disagree with what he is saying. Could I, even if I don't like it? He's Jesus. This just isn't what I expected. I have a lot to learn.

"Exactly."

Wait, did He just respond to my thoughts, or was He repeating Himself? That's unnerving.

"Don't worry, everyone thinks that."

I draw in a slow breath. "Okay… so how do I get this started? I don't want to waste any more time than I need to here."

He smiles. "Always the go-getter. We start with you and what you've done." He paused, "And didn't do. Then we heal. You heal. One relationship at a time heals."

"How many people?"

"As many as it takes."

"So, this is how I'm going to spend eternity then?"

He chuckles. "No, it takes as long as it takes, but not eternity. It may seem like forever but that's only when you get impatient. Just remember, whatever it takes to get back to Peia right?"

"Wait, what happens to people who don't do this?"

"They don't heal. They don't enter into communion with us. They... usually, come around... eventually. It's a tough battle to go through alone so We're always there waiting."

"Where do we start?"

"Don't lose what's important to you in this process. That's not what this is about. It's only about healing. Let's take a rest. Then we can talk about Peia."

We are back at the church. I feel like I'm going to be sick, so I sit in a nearby chair. I quickly jump to the next one when I hear groaning from the chair. The first chair may be at the end of its usefulness. I am examining its structural integrity when I realize Jesus isn't next to me. I look for Him and finally spot Him. Jesus is sitting in a back pew this time, His arms folded behind His head.

"Felt like a change of scenery?" I tease.

Jesus smiles and drops His arms to His side.

"I never did this for attention. I kinda like sitting back and watching sometimes." He adds, "You can learn a lot from the people who try to slip in unnoticed. If you're patient with them."

I think about when I first went to church on my own and tried to go unnoticed.

"You've just got to find where you belong," I say dreamily.

Jesus smiles, "A prophet is not—"

"Welcome in their home town," we finish the verse together.

His eyes twinkle and I start to wonder what He's up to.

"Now, My child," He says, "we have work to do."

Chapter 8

"Triumph, all ye cherubim,
Sing with us, ye seraphim,
Heaven and earth resound the hymn:
Salve, salve, salve Regina!

To thee we cry, poor sons of Eve,
O Maria!
To thee we sigh, we mourn, we grieve,
O Maria!"

Hail Holy Queen

CATHERINE

It is early when I decide to check my phone. My heart sinks when I see the voicemail icon. I check my voicemail and my heart jumps to my throat when I hear my dad's shaky voice say, "Call me as soon as you get this... it's about Mom."
This isn't supposed to happen yet. She was doing better.
I sit up and blink the last sleepiness out of my eyes. I go into the living room so I don't wake Tim. I call my dad back and he picks up after the second ring.

"Honey, your mom died last night—er—or this morning. At 2 AM."

"I'm so sorry, Dad."

"We're taking care of things here… we don't know when the funeral will be yet… probably the end of the week. Can you make it back?"

"Yeah, of course! I'll check with work to be sure, but I'll be there. Is there anything I can do for you?"

"I… no."

I can hear that he needs something, but it's something I can't give. He just lost the person he loved for almost 50 years. What could anyone possibly do to fill that?

The rest of the conversation blurs and is little more than a murmur.

Things change around Jesus and I. We're in the house I grew up in. I'm much younger than most of these memories, around twelve. I am looking at boxes and thumbing through a cookbook in the kitchen. I have no idea what I'm doing, but I want to try. Mom glides in but instantly frowns.

"What mess are you starting?" she asks.

"I—I just wanted to try to make some muffins or something," I stammer. I want to try a recipe, not just the box mix.

She takes the cookbook and puts it away.

"Just use this." She hands me the box mix. "It's easier."

She wanders out of the room again.

The room is somehow lonelier now as I'm alone again.

I sigh and look at the directions. '*Easier isn't what I'm looking for,*' I think to myself.

Things change again. We're at the hospital. Grace is handed to me, pink and wrinkly when she stops screaming; I can see her shining eyes. She coos and my eyes fill with tears. They do again, just watching this. She's perfect. I long for her, but I can't. I wish for her a long, full, and happy life, not a quick entry here. If I could spare her this place, I would.

"You would do anything for her. You will see her—don't worry, time is irrelevant here, remember? She could live for 100 years and you will see her soon."

The scene changes. We're at home. Grace is a little older, but not much. I am lying in bed. I'm…

"You were in pain."

"I was sad—I… I needed to be stronger."

"Grief is pain."

"I'm sorry I failed her."

"That's not why we're here."

Tim puts Grace on the bed next to me. "I know you're hurting, but Catherine, she needs you." Tim's voice breaks just the tiniest bit. The loss has been hard on him too, but mostly the way I can't seem to cope with it.

Grace crawls over to me giggling and I can't help but laugh through my tears. She pulls at my hair, but not hard. She puts her head on the bed as if to start a headstand and giggles.

"I know," I respond and pull her close into my embrace. I can't believe I could ignore her over something so small. I mean *this* baby I can hold and I need to be here for her, even when I'm hurting.

I'm at a hospital now. We're in the hallway and there is a Madonna holding baby Jesus tenderly in her arms. The intricate detail of her face shows her love and devotion to her child. I look down the hallway, but I don't recognize the hospital.

"In here," Jesus says, pointing to a room.

"Then why? Oh, never mind." I walk over to where He is pointing. It's an operating room and a woman is on the table. My mother is lying there, under anesthesia, the beeping of machines all around her, nurses and the doctor scurrying to and fro. I know I'm not really here, but I'm scared to enter the room and see it. Suddenly the beeping intensifies.

"We have to do it now!" the doctor says.

There is more scurrying, and suddenly there is a little gasp. After a little more hurried motions, a baby wailing.

"This was my birth."

"Yes."

It is then I turn and notice a priest beside me by the glass window watching, praying over my mother and me.

"He stays with you both through the night. It is a rough one for both of you."

"My mom told me," I say quietly. Then I turn to Jesus, a little embarrassed. "Did he really give me last rites? I mean what a way to start out life, expecting to die."

Jesus smiles. "You were anointed at birth to bring strength and healing," He says as he takes my hands in His, "to yourself, and to others."

"That's why I became a nurse."

"Partly, you could have taken many paths to accomplish this calling. It did look like you chose a good one for you." He smiles. My face burns with embarrassment and with pride.

BRICE

We're at the hospital. Sophie is in labor and I am right there beside her. I am ashamed I can't tell which of the boys is coming, Jax or Devin. I scan the room and my memory for any detail that would give it away, but nothing stands out to me. I watch patiently and do my best to support Sophie. If I could take this pain from her I would, but I also know it is a pain I could never bear. I am in awe of her strength and determination and even now, I love her more than I thought possible for it.

I finally see it when he is born: it's Jax, it's our firstborn. Jax, son of Jack, well sort of, my middle name being Jackson. He is beautiful. He is amazing. Sophie falls back onto the bed exhausted as the nurse hands him to her. A light seems to shine from her. A halo I think. She is the mother of my children, my wife, and my soulmate. I yearn to see her again as a tear streams down my cheek.

Suddenly the scene changes. I am sitting on a counter kicking my feet. I couldn't be more than five years old. I'm not very helpful in the kitchen, but I like being here. Everyone says I'm cute. The people look a little different; some look like they have been playing outside really hard. Mom gets mad at me when I'm that dirty. I wonder why she looks at them differently, she isn't angry, but I don't know what it is in her eyes instead...

"Pity, I see it now, she pitied them."

"Yes, which is unfortunate, but her intent was good. She taught you early to feed my people."

"Yeah." I am panged with guilt and worry. I wonder if I can visit her. I don't think it's time to ask though.

We're at my childhood home and I'm a little older, but I don't remember anything special about this day. Everyone going about their morning routine seems completely normal.

I turn to Jesus. "What... I don't understand why we are here. If now, then why not every moment of every day?"

He laughs a little. "Sometimes the little things become the big things, but you're right, we won't comb through every second of your life. Maybe this will help." He points to my mom.

She stops what she was doing at the counter and sits in a chair nearby. "I can't believe I forgot."

"Forgot what, Mom?" I ask. Dad and Bryan are already out the door, so they don't hear her.

"I forgot it was the day my mom died." Her face is ashen and she looks like she is about to cry. "Next I'll probably forget her birthday!" Now she does break into tears.

I'm not sure what to say to comfort her. I didn't meet my grandma, or I was too young to remember, but I know that's not what she needs to hear right now. I wish I had something I could say or do to make this better.

"I'm sorry, Mom." Then, the problem solver I am, I say, "Can I write it down? So we don't forget again?"

She turns to me as if she finally notices I'm there. "Okay, Brice." And she smiles a little. Maybe I did actually fix things, but she still looks so lonely.

I look to Jesus for some deep insight. I mean this was sad and all; maybe I did the right thing. I'm not really sure what else there was to be done.

He smiles and relief washes over me. "You showed kindness when she needed it. Sometimes we allow the people we love to walk with us, even after they die. Sometimes, we carry the grief of their absence as an impossible burden." He quickly adds, "Neither is wrong, but one does make things harder."

"How do we know which we are doing?"

"By the weight of the grief."

CATHERINE

I am sitting in a small pew, in a small chapel, not really sure why I wandered into this place. I laugh at my own awkwardness. I had no idea then what I was getting into, but now I am so glad I did. I watch my younger self fidget with my coat, unwilling to take it off; can't show I'm staying. Or maybe I feel underdressed in my t-shirt and jeans as I spot a sister with her black and white habit. A few other people amble in and I do not feel so underdressed. They are nearby ranchers and such and all in jeans and boots, though they are also very tidy. They seem to not bring a speck of dirt with them, though they must have been working outside all day. I feel like such a city girl in comparison.

A sister enters and starts to play the organ. In a moment, the others start to file in two at a time. It's relaxing to know I'm in a memory that isn't so sad or painful.

"I've told you this isn't about pain and punishment."

"No, this time it's about faith."

"It's always about faith."

Around us, things are different, yet they are the same.

We're at the abbey again. This time I'm outside, working with the sisters on pulling weeds. It is a cheerful, though brisk, mountain morning. It isn't hard work except for the size of the field and the monotony of it. I'm not alone in the field, but we are spread out working to clear spots here and there. The sun pops out from behind a cloud and the warmth is refreshing in the cool dewy morning.

I stare at the scene for a long time waiting for something to happen but I'm not sure what I'm waiting for.

"Your prayer was just so beautiful here. I like being in moments like this. I know you feel me more," Jesus says.

The younger me wipes sweat from my brow. The sun is starting to beat down on us now. We are just finishing up and will head over to the main building for some prayer.

"Oh, I see, the prayers that the sisters lead inside. That's what we're here to see."

"No." He sighs a little, but doesn't seem disappointed. "The work was your prayer. Remember the saying they had, work is prayer and prayer is work. This, this prayer was a beautiful act of kindness."

The cows take over the field now that we have left and opened a gate for them. They happily munch down on the grass and sage that we left behind.

"I haven't thought about that in years."

"I know," is all He says, and then we are gone again.

BRICE

We're in a different hospital room. One I don't recognize. The decor is fairly dated so it must be around the time I was... and recognition washes over me. That is my mom in the hospital bed. This must be when I was born.

"I couldn't possibly have done anything wrong here?"

"No," is His only response.

"I don't think I have any painful memories either, I mean, I don't remember this."

"No."

"It... Okay, I'll admit it. I don't know why we are here."

"This is the day I called you."

"You called me?"

"Yes."

"To do what?"

"To bring healing and strength to the world."

I am already feeling like a disappointment, but I ask, "And did I?"

The smile of pride on Jesus' face brought tears to my eyes. "Yes, yes, my child, you did."

We're at the temple, and I instantly realize what day it is. How could I forget? It is when Sophie and I get married. I don't see myself though, instead I'm in the room with Sophie.

"I'm nervous," she says to her mom.

"I know, but you've come this far. You are ready." She smiles.

"I know. He's a good man," she says, blushing. "He'll be a good husband. And father. I just… is it really going to last forever?"

"It will if you work on it. Love takes effort," her mom says. "It is more than warm fuzzy feelings. Those are nice, but… it definitely takes two. It's more like it happens between two people than something inside of you."

"But what if—is this all I'll ever be?" She looks down then back up at her mother. "Someone's wife?"

I walk up to Sophie and reach up to touch her cheek but drop my hand sadly.

"I wish I could tell you how much I miss you," I whisper to her. "You could never be only my wife, or anyone's."

We're at a nursing home this time. The one my mom was in; the one my mom died in. We walk down the hall and there are some religious statues or something as well as the pictures on the wall. I wasn't close to my mom after my baptism so I didn't really have any involvement in her care or choosing this place. I get to her room and pause outside the door with the flowers I brought her. What if this is the same as it has been? All I can do is try.

I open the door and my brother and dad are in the room. A woman I don't know is standing next to Bryan and comes over to me and hugs me.

"You must be Brice," she says. "I'm Bryan's wife, Julie."

I'm shocked at this, but then we never were close, Bryan and I, so why would I know about her?

The flowers are already in a vase, so I put them by the others on a table a few feet from the bed. My dad tries to rouse Mom. "Honey, he's here. Brice is here."

She opens her eyes, but they roll back into her head almost immediately. The tubes and wires around her hooked to monitors and machines beeping and sighing make her look almost like something from one of my science fiction movies I love to watch. Almost. The scene is surreal, yet the pain in my chest tells me it is actually more real than anything else I have felt. I sit next to the bed but still on the side by the door. I won't let my escape be blocked off that easily. I reach for her hand, then hesitate. Do I even belong here anymore? While I am thinking, she sighs and moves her hand in her sleep. It settles into my hand, answering my question.

I squeeze her hand and say, "Hi, Mom." My voice cracks a little but I continue, "I know it's been a while, but—but I'm here now."

The sighing of the machine helping her breathe continues.

It is sometime later, hours I think, but we are there in an instant.

"Time isn't the same here," Jesus says. I jump. I forgot that I wasn't alone watching the scenes of my life playing out before me. "You all seem to forget you are not alone." He smiles at me then turns back.

I open my mouth to say something to him, but I am interrupted by a sigh and then a long beep. My mom has breathed her last breath. She is gone.

We are back at the church, but I am still wondering where these pieces of my life fall into this process of moving on. I look around, but do not initially see Jesus.

I notice something different on the sacramental table, something bright red. I approach and find an apple sitting there next to the bread. I look at the shiny scarlet peel and my mind wanders back to the Garden of Eden. Did Eve know what she was getting into? In the Sunday lessons I was told she did, that she chose this life for all of us so that we can truly grow and know God. I look up and see gentle, but bright eyes staring back at me.

"Yes, I did. I did it for you, so you could be free to grow, to take this path even though you fall." Her eyes are shining with tears even though she is smiling.

"Eve," I whisper, still amazed at this apparition before me.

"Have courage, my child, as I once did," she kisses my forehead gently, then she is gone.

I am standing alone again and down at the apple on the table. I turn and scan the room carefully. I know He is here somewhere.

"You know it is a little frustrating trying to track you down every five minutes," I say when I find Jesus laying across a pew.

"But you always know I'll be here somewhere," He says mockingly.

"Of course, you'll be in your Father's house," I tease back.

He sits and grows more serious. "There are always a few parts of your life where you will seem to be alone—you won't see me—but it's like life. I'm with you even if you can't see me."

I am troubled by His words, but I take a deep breath; I must walk by faith.

Chapter 9

"Redeem the years I've thrown away
I'm ready to make good on what I've
wasted

I'm asking You to shape my heart
I want to be Your work of art
'Cause when You change me
And make me more like You"

It's Beautiful by Eleventyseven

CATHERINE

We're... it's... it's after I got sick. I'm starting to lose my hair and my cheekbones are more prominent. It was such a humbling experience. I realized I could be a jerk sometimes, so I am trying to be kinder. I know I'm not going to earn my way into heaven in a last dash effort, but I mean, it couldn't hurt, right?
"Did you have a run-in with a razor?" someone chuckles, but I just put my head down and hurry on my way.
It was early on in losing my hair, so I didn't get the pity looks from people... yet.

I see a family across the restaurant. I never liked the parents and I didn't know their boys, but I remember their daughter. I knew her from my days as a nurse, before my illness became my only existence. There was a sparkle about that girl I can't quite describe. I miss her though I didn't know her well. I wish… I wish I had been able to help her more. I say a little prayer for her. I don't even know if I remember her name now, but I remember her birthday. Dates of birth are a big deal in confirming the patient identity and it dawns on me, the family is out to dinner today because it is her birthday. I take a big drink of my water to force the lump in my throat down and I flag down my waitress.

"I want to pay for their meal," I say and point to Brice and Sophie. I'll never be their friends, but it's the least I can do, for their daughter. "Anonymously though."

"Of course," she says as she winks. "Random act of kindness. Love it!" she squeals.

The scene melts around us again. I'm in the hospital now.

It's a slow walk down the corridor. I place each foot carefully. If I were to fall in this weakened state, it would really be the end of the world; or at least the end of me. One foot, then the other, then the walker; one foot, then the other, then the walker.

A woman appears around a corner, careful to make a wide circle. Does she think she'll catch leukemia if I touch her? I want to lean over and cough on her, but the patronizing pity on her face makes me gag. Great, I can puke on her, much more contaminating. I'm finally almost past her when she lets out a big sneeze.

"Bless you," I say automatically.

"I'm… Oh, God!" she says, and she actually runs full speed the rest of the way down the hall. It dawns on me. She wasn't scared of catching anything. She's scared of what she'll give me; scared she'll kill me with a cold. I stop walking.

"I'm sure it was nothing," says the nurse beside me. "If you want to be done today, I'm sure it's fine." She pats my arm tenderly.

"I'm fine," I brace my walker even tighter. I hate how everyone treats me like I'm so fragile. I'm not a porcelain doll. I'm stronger than this.

I take another step, then another, then shift the walker. One more, I tell myself. Just one at a time, then it's like nothing. I can handle one more. Then one more. Step, step, walker, step, step, walker. If I just stay focused, I'll make it. My throat is tight, but I ignore it. Step, step, but something is wrong…

"Oh," the nurse squeaks, then quickly, "Help over here! I think she's blacking out!"

Sure enough, blackness is washing over my vision as I start to crumple toward the ground. Maybe it was one too many after all.

I awake in my hospital bed surrounded by concerned faces. I want to say I'm fine, but "Mmm-hmm," is all I manage to mumble.

"You need to rest," a voice says sternly, but relief is clearly washing over the doctor's face. It's one of the on-calls, not Dr. Phillips, my oncologist. I stopped learning the on-calls' names two days ago. There are too many, and they don't seem to take the time to learn my name either.

"Fine." I am even surprised my voice works this time. I close my eyes and wait for the whispering and shuffling to leave, but they are apparently in no hurry. I shift and wriggle a little to get more comfortable. A nurse checks my pulse and blood pressure on one side. The doctor on the other orders some medicine or something. I also stopped paying attention to the names of the medications weeks ago. I only listen to the side effects now. As I said, if the cancer doesn't kill me, the chemo surely will.

A nurse fiddles with something next to me for a few moments, then I hear her footsteps retreat across the room. I breathe out a deep sigh. How can I rest when they won't leave?

Something cold surges into my arm from the IV. It is a shock to my system, but I soon acclimate to the new sensation. An ache I didn't notice until it is gone fades away along with the coldness. As the pain lifts, my eyelids grow heavy. Sounds fade as either they leave or I fall asleep. Curious, I'm not sure which is happening...

"We need to clean your chemo port—oh sorry"—her voice softens—"I didn't realize you were still sleeping. I can come back."

"It's okay." I sit up. "Do what you need to."

She starts with washing her hands and putting on fresh gloves with a snap, then comes the face mask. She sits on the rolling stool next to my bed and brings it closer along with the tray beside her. She arranges a few things on her tray. I pull my gown down exposing the port but trying to keep as much modesty as I can. It is so difficult for the infirmed to keep our dignity. I am already nauseous from the chemo; this process and especially the pungent smells are sickening, so I look away and try my best not to breathe through my nose or even too deeply through my mouth.

"Almost done," she says kindly. And then, "There you go dear," as she scoots away, tearing off her gloves with another snap. The ache has returned even though the IV is still dripping beside me.

The nurse is just leaving when she ducks her head back. "Try to keep the faith. You're on the donor list. They're searching the registry. A bone marrow match is bound to turn up soon." She smiles as she disappears again.

"Keep the faith," I sigh. "More like make peace with it. And any final arrangements," I scoff. People just have to find some kind of silver lining, but that isn't always possible.

BRICE

I notice a woman stumbling out of the restaurant I am about to walk by. At first, I look to see if I can cross the street to avoid her. She's obviously drunk and I recognize her as one of those mean girls from high school. She's probably a mean drunk too, so best to get away unnoticed. When I see my opportunity to cross, I look back at her and my heart softens in spite of my obvious danger of being tainted by her lack of moral compass. Some people you can't help but feel sorry for; even if it's their own fault. I come up behind her but try to shuffle my feet and almost stomp so I don't startle her.

"Do you need a hand, Miss?" My attempt at warning her of my presence didn't work and she nearly topples over in surprise. I manage to help her catch her balance.

"Well, helllll-oooo," she stammers, attempting to flutter her eyelashes but laughing at her own failure to do so correctly.

"Where are you headed?" I just hope she isn't going far.

"Round the corner," she slurs. "Just a house or two down." She looks at her fingers counting one, two, and back again like she is trying to make up her mind which it is: one or two?

"That's right, you moved into Brown's old place."

"Ya betcha," she says, abandoning her attempt at counting.

We stumble away and I flush when I see a fellow church member cross our path. I'm not guilty by association. I just don't want her to fall on her face.

As we disappear around the corner, I say to Jesus, "Are we going to follow?"

"No, that's all we needed really," Jesus says.

"So we're done here." I shuffle my foot, using it to play with a pile of dust in front of me.

"Yes." And we are back at the church. Out of the corner of my eye, I notice a picture ajar on the wall next to me. I turn and straighten it. It is a picture of Jesus walking with His cross and someone is next to Him. Odd, this doesn't belong here; we focus on His life, not His death. I have never seen a cross in the chapel. I turn back to Jesus standing before me, but as I do the picture falls from its hook and crashes to the floor, making me wince.

CATHERINE

We are back in the church. I don't see Jesus, so I walk along the east wall. Half of the Stations of the Cross are hung here with great stained-glass windows above them. The west wall facing me has almost a mirror image of the wall next to me with the other half of the Stations. After walking past a few pews, I am startled to find Jesus lying down in a pew. I don't want to disturb His rest, so I sit by His feet, careful not to touch them.

As I hear the gentle rise and fall of His breath, I look around. There isn't much to focus on besides the clutter. I try to wait patiently, but it is hard to be patient when my soul is on the line. I look over at the wall beside me. The Stations of the Cross are like three-dimensional pictures, a mix of a carving and painting. They are carved out of a light, fragrant wood. I am mesmerized by the intricate detail of the carving. I stand again and walk closer. I reach up, but I am scared to touch the sacred artwork; especially in a place that is falling apart around me. I remember attending Stations of the Cross with my devout mother, but I still can't recall them all. This one depicts Jesus and His cross along with another man. "Simone the Cyrene," I whisper as it comes back to me. Jesus stirs and sits up behind me. As I turn back to Him, I notice the first four stations have fallen off the wall.

"I'm ready now, I think." Jesus smiles as He stretches.

We're back in my memories now. I'm in the hospital going through an especially difficult round of chemo. Everyone says it's bad, but few know how bad some treatments really are. If the disease doesn't kill you, the treatment will. I am lying on the bed with tubes and wires all around connected to all sorts of things beeping, buzzing, sighing, and humming. The port in my chest is currently connected to the machine, though I can only take it for so long. Soon it will have to be disconnected to give me a slight reprieve, but now... now it is burning through my veins, testing my pain threshold, searing nerves until I wish for numbness again. Pain like this makes me long for the oblivion of addiction in spite of myself. I know better than to wish that back onto myself. Time seems to stand still and fly by at the same time. It is difficult to tell between the unending pain, the isolation of disease, and the monotony of the hospital.

Finally, a visitor appears. My husband has come to visit after work. However, I am in too much pain to notice the change around me. I writhe on the bed, wincing at every touch of the sheet. When I look at Tim, I see my pain reflected in his eyes. The profound helplessness of not being able to take away or soothe my agony. He stays by my side though and we are together in our own isolated existence, my pain, and his helplessness.

Jesus and I visit another memory, this time of remission. I am home with Tim and Grace. Things are almost normal, almost. I am able to do most of the things I love, though it is tiring. I am tending a few indoor plants in our sunroom. I walk over with a watering can, but after a few minutes, I sit again to catch my breath. I am determined to finish the task, so I start again, but again can only last a few minutes before needing a break. Grace appears in the doorway. "Let me do that, Mom, you need to—we're just happy you're home, you don't need to..."

"Thank you, but I want to"—I take a breath—"I need to"—another breath—"feel useful."

She walks in and wraps her arms tenderly around me. "You are useful. Just being here. Just—just getting healthy again."

"You know what's healthy?" I breathe deeply and continue, "Plants. They need me. I—and I need them."

"Okay, Mom," she says, only slightly condescending, and she rises to leave. From the doorway, she adds tenderly, "Classes don't start again for a week, so if you need anything before then, I'm here." She adds some emphasis this time. "*Anything*."

I smile and rise again to continue watering.

Just like that, I'm back at the cathedral.

"I miss her so. I—mean I don't wish her to be here. She deserves a long, *long*, happy life," I say. "I—I wish I could see what she's up to now. I don't know how long I've been gone. I don't know how her wedding was, how her marriage is, does she have kids? How is her career? Can I—do we really get to—look down from here and check on them?" I finally dredge up the courage to ask, but I am afraid of the answer.

Jesus walks across the church and heaves His shoulder under a rather large slab of plaster from the ceiling, now sprawled across three fragmented pews.

"A hand?" His strained voice asks meekly. "Please." The need in the plea is genuine.

I hurry over but stop just short, unsure where to lift. "How… I'm not…" I'm not that strong. I walk around it, weighing my options.

"Here." Jesus lifts His right hand and points.

I hurry over and gingerly place my left shoulder under it, taking as much weight as I think I can manage.

"Closer," He says firmly, but compassionately.

I inch over, groaning under the weight. This has got to be too much for me.

"One… Two… Three!"

"Wait, what?" but it is already tipping behind us, so I try to follow the momentum. I lose my balance a little but catch myself only to stub my toe in the process. A cloud of dust overpowers me just as I'm sucking in a deep wince from the pain. I cough, my eyes full of tears and the blinding light from a sudden shock of pain. A hand slaps my back and I sputter and eventually can breathe again. Jesus' smiling face comes into focus again.

"We did it." He cocks His head slightly, beaming with pride.

"Yes, we did." The warm feeling of satisfaction swells deep inside.

BRICE

I am oddly nervous as I walk up to the podium at the front of the church. It's different seeing myself from the back of the chapel, yet I know my every thought. Each step takes immense effort and I can't seem to breathe right. The lump in my throat... I just can't swallow. Most faces are turned forward, away from me, waiting. I can feel the nervousness off others too. Row after row, waiting intently for what I have to say. My wife and children, my friends, my neighbors, even some new people I don't recognize. This could be the reason they come back. Or don't. No pressure.

"Don't be nervous," someone whispers to me as I pass.

I hate it when people say that. They may as well tell me to not breathe. I feel the way I feel and at this moment, I feel nervous. These people who say things like, 'don't be nervous,' may as well tell me to not be myself. Just stop being so... Brice. It also doesn't help that when people tell me to stop being nervous, I focus on how nervous I am all the more. I wish I could just turn my nerves off. Really I do, but that isn't a skill I have learned.

I reach the podium and must try to not be so Brice, or at least not so nervous. I settle my notes. My hands tremble slightly as I try one last time to clear my throat. Come on, Brice, you've done this a dozen times now. This is nothing special.

"Brothers and Sisters," I begin. "Today's lesson is about hardship.

"Mosiah 24: 8-15.

"And now it came to pass that Amulon began to exercise authority over Alma and his brethren, and began to persecute him, and cause that his children should persecute their children. For Amulon knew Alma, that he had been one of the king's priests, and that it was he that believed the words of Abinadi and was driven out before the king, and therefore he was wroth with him; for he was subject to king Laman, yet he exercised authority over them, and put tasks upon them, and put task-masters over them. And it came to pass that so great were their afflictions that they began to cry mightily to God. And Amulon commanded them that they should stop their cries; and he put guards over them to watch them, that whosoever should be found calling upon God should be put to death. And Alma and his people did not raise their voices to the Lord their God, but did pour out their hearts to him; and he did know the thoughts of their hearts. And it came to pass that the voice of the Lord came to them in their afflictions, saying: Lift up your heads and be of good comfort, for I know of the covenant which ye have made unto me; and I will covenant with my people and deliver them out of bondage. And I will also ease the burdens which are put upon your shoulders, that even you cannot feel them upon your backs, even while you are in bondage; and this will I do that ye may stand as witnesses for me hereafter and that ye may know of a surety that I, the Lord God, do visit my people in their afflictions. And now it came to pass that the burdens which were laid upon Alma and his brethren were made light; yea, the Lord did strengthen them that they could bear up their burdens with ease, and they did submit cheerfully and with patience to all the will of the Lord.

"I think what strikes me the most is how when we ask God to help us, we can get more than we bargain for—"

Chuckles abound from the congregation, but not too raucous.

I continue, "They asked for the burdens of life to be lighter, but that isn't His plan for us. We can't take the easy path and have strong faith, a strong heart. See I believe faith and love have to be strengthened just as much as our muscles. We stretch as far as we can and we are asked to go just a little farther, always give just a little more, love just a little more dearly. The burdens of life are heavy because they are love. Love of one, love of all. When we recognize that, the weight isn't so bad. We simply need the strength to bear it.

In the Name of Jesus Christ, Amen."

I return to my seat and the service continues in a blur. I turn to Jesus beside me.

"That was the last time I spoke at a service. I died a few days later," I say slowly. It makes my words so much heavier than I intended.

114

Jesus is standing at the back of the chapel near a painting of the Last Supper. I try to see what is so important; it's just a painting. My sadness quickly turns to anger.

"Do you know why I chose twelve disciples? Why I chose those disciples?" Jesus asks me as He reaches up and touches the face of Peter in the painting.

"It was symbolic. Twelve tribes of Israel. I think something about twelve representing perfect leadership…"

"No." He smiles, but there is a longing in His expression. "They were my friends—my best friends." He looks deeply into my eyes and I feel incredibly lonely.

"I've never had friends like that," I manage to say before I clear the lump from my throat.

"I know," He says and hugs me.

After a while, He lets go of me and quietly walks across the chapel. A section of the wall has collapsed. I avert my eyes from its clear signs of degradation. Finally, a groan from the right draws my attention. I stand and carefully pick my way around broken chairs and piles of plaster. I get around the chairs and finally see Him. He has His shoulder under a piece of the wall trying to lift it off the long back table and broken chairs.

"Why? I—I mean it's such a mess, what's the point?" I realize how miserable I sound.

"We have to start somewhere," He says with a half-smile.

I go around to the other side of the broken wall, sizing it up. I try a couple of spots only to have them crumple at the slightest pressure.

"I'm… I'm not sure I can," I mutter, defeated.

"Try… there." He points a little ahead of Himself. I pick myself up and place myself carefully where I think He suggests, but it crumbles.

"To the left a little… a little more… there, that should work better."

I follow His directions and reposition myself as best I can. I am barely in place when I hear Him say, "One… two… three!"

We both heave, though I feel like my contributions are minimal to the effort. The wall topples, slides, and finally flips in a cloud of dust and plaster. Jesus claps the dust off His hands, also wiping them on His thighs to be sure the dust is off them.

"Now what?" He asks as He turns to me.

Chapter 10

"Lord, lift the veil that clouds my vision,
Loose ev'ry chain and inhibition.
More than a prayer it's my decision
To break this heart, O God
with what breaks your heart, O God.
Please, break my heart

For the sick, for the poor,
For the ones who need more
Tenderness and justice,
Break my heart
For the lost, for the lame
For those suff'ring in pain
Help me see you in each face
through a broken heart"

Break My Heart by Jennifer Martin

CATHERINE

I'm at the hospital. It's been a rough night already. I walk to the nurse's station to sit for a moment. I put down the files in my hands and put my head in them instead.

"Why do I do this?" I say to myself. It's like I'm a nurse because I'm always making up for something. I'm… I'm apologizing for existing, I realize as I look at my younger self.

The call light starts flashing. I groan, but I take a deep breath to regain my composure. Room 6, I read off the display and head over there.

The ER is still a bustle, so I have to weave around a few coworkers attending to other patients. I reach the room and glance up through the glass door. The curtain is open a little, but I can just see the occupant of the bed. A sweet little girl is lying there on the bed, looking nervously around her. I smile before opening the sliding door and go through the opening in the curtain.

"Hello," I say to her and I look around for her parent. "My name is Catherine, I'm a nurse. Did your mom or dad step out?"

"Yeah, my mom needed to call my dad. She'll be right back, but that's not why…" she trails off, looking down.

"Well then," I sit on the rolling stool. "What can I do to help you?"

"I'm… I'm afraid," her voice quivers. "I know mom will be back I just… never mind. I'm a big girl. I'm five!" she quickly adds.

"You are," I say, showing I'm impressed. "In fact, I bet you can keep me company."

"Oh?"

"Yeah, I've had a pretty long night," I say honestly.

"Really?" she says excitedly. "So I can help you?" Her eyes squint. She's not buying it. Not yet.

"Absolutely," I say, then scrunch my eyebrows seriously. "It is a hard job being a nurse. I take temperatures and blood pressure." I make a face, "Sometimes, I even have to draw blood. It gets exhausting." I sigh, but add, "But I love what I do. I get to help people. I get to see people get healthy again. And sometimes, I even get to have fun." I pull my pen and pad of paper out of my pocket, "Do you by chance know tic-tac-toe?"

"Yes," she laughs as I draw the game grid.

"So what's wrong here?" I ask Jesus.

"Nothing," He says.

I look at myself laughing and playing with the little girl, but a sadness washes over me.

"She died, sometime later... I can't remember exactly, but she—she did, didn't she?" I say, crying.

"Yes," He says solemnly.

"I couldn't save her," I whimper, but then I see that Jesus is crying too. "You... you look sad?"

"Psalm 116:15: 'How painful it is to the Lord when one of his people dies!'" Jesus says.

I nod and am quiet, waiting for the insight or whatever He has planned.

He walks over to the girl and puts a hand on her shoulder. She smiles and looks vaguely in His direction. He smiles in return.

He walks over to me. "It's time to go," He says, still smiling.

"See you later," the little girl says so quietly I can barely hear, and she looks right at me like she can see me.

Puzzled I turn to go with Jesus just as the mother is stepping back into the room. She was right outside it and I hadn't noticed her.

"Sorry, Peia. Oh, thanks," she mumbles. "You can go," she adds a little more sternly.

The younger me rolls my eyes after I pass her.

The scene of trying to encourage Peia repeats in my mind.

When I look up again, Jesus is sitting, leaning against an intact pillar. I go to rest beside Him. He wipes His sweaty brow with His arm, but it only smears dust into the sweat and blood. I smile and say, "Let me." I have nothing but my tunic and my hands are just as dirty as His. I tear off a piece from the bottom, by my knee. I look at Jesus and He smiles His agreement. I rise to my knees, fumble with the cloth for a moment, and then gently wipe His cheeks up and across His brow. I am finishing, and as the cloth dangles in front of His face, He sighs in relief, and with a hand, He presses the whole cloth to His face. After a few seconds, He lowers His hand and I pull my cloth away but drop it in front of me: His face is perfectly copied onto the fabric.

"Just like Veronica," I mumble as I pick the cloth up again.

BRICE

"Daddy?"

"Yes, Peia?" I answer her.

"I have a question… but I'm not sure how you will answer," she says coyly.

I look deeply into her sky-blue eyes. "Honestly. As always, as honestly as I can," I assure her.

"Would I still be me if…"

I am a little confused. "I can't imagine anything that could change who you are, my Sweet Pea."

She looks at me very seriously now. "Dad, but would I still be me if… if I was… normal? If… if I didn't have Down's syndrome? Would I still be… me?" She looks away at the last part of her question.

"I…of course… you would." More confidently, I add, "You are Cassiopeia. You were chosen by God to be my daughter."

"I know," she sighs, clearly frustrated, "but would I be *me*?"

Suddenly, I'm back at the chapel. A demon with orange eyes peaks over a chair. Annoyed, I turn away and focus on the debris in front of me. I see the critter run across the room, without much interest from me. It hops quickly onto the chair by the sacrament table. I grab a piece of wood from a nearby broken pew and run at the table.

"Go away!" I shout, and the fat demon pulls its paw back and cowers. I continue to advance and it panics, squeaks and falls off the chair. It looks like a turtle on its fat back. I can't help but chuckle at the sight. It manages to flip right-side-up and hurries away. I am left chuckling at the clumsy, fat demon.

CATHERINE

"It's good news, Catherine. It's in remission."
My eyes fill with tears of joy as I cover my mouth. I don't want to scream, but I want to scream.
"I…" I can't find the words. I don't think I have heard three sweeter words. It's in remission! It's gone. It's really gone. I'm crying.
"I don't want to diminish your joy—" Dr. Phillips interjects.
"No, of course, whatever it is. I want to hear it. Be completely honest," I respond.
"There is a chance of recurrence. It may come back someday," the doctor says.
I suck in a deep, slow breath. That is a killjoy.
"Okay. I will be ready if it does and—I just…" I start to cry again. "I could kiss you." I blush. "But I won't of course." I laugh nervously. I don't know why I said that.
Luckily the doctor laughs too. "I do hear that sometimes." Then he adds solemnly, "On good days. Well, congratulations." He stands up and heads for the door. "We'll do a follow up in six months."
"So what? I didn't appreciate my second chance at life?" I turn to Jesus. "Or is this just a tease? I mean it did come *back*." I can't hide my touch of bitterness in that last word.
Jesus smiles just as sweetly as ever and simply says, "Wait and see."
"Okay, and what, pray tell, am I looking for?"

He simply points.

I'm leaving Dr. Phillips's office now and I walk out into the lobby. I almost run the poor thing over. She can't be older than ten and looks quite gaunt, though sweet as ever under her sullen expression.

"I'm sorry," I say kindly.

"It's okay," she says, looking down miserably. She must be miserable if she's going into this office.

I bend down so I can look her in the eyes. "There are angels in that office, you know."

"Really?" She perks up, but then disbelief sets in. "They're just people."

"Well, yes," I resolve, shifting on my knee uncomfortably. "But sometimes they work miracles. Try… try to have faith in them. It will be okay."

I stand to go as I hear a mumbled, "Thanks" from her parents. Funny I didn't pay attention to them when I stopped to talk to her. I slightly regret stopping and talking to her when I look at them.

"Brice. Sophie. I—I'm sorry," I spit out and I turn to leave. Their daughter has grown, and it appears has had a heavy burden over the past several years.

Watching the memory, I turn to Jesus. "So? What, I didn't comfort her enough? Didn't say the right thing? What do I need to atone for now?"

"This isn't about atonement, my child." We're back at the cathedral now. Jesus walks over to the Stations of the Cross, but I've had enough. I sit in the nearest pew and turn away. I just can't do this right now; I'm only human.

A bird-like creature appears from a shadow above me. It seems like a cross between a crow and a peacock standing with proud shoulders held high. It is all black with a small but fancy-looking tail. Its eyes are deep purple and striking against its dark face. This doesn't look like something I want as a pet, and yet I am mesmerized by the creature's clear vanity.

BRICE

I am sitting at a table in the food court at the mall. I think I'm a teenager from how I look, but I can't be sure. It looks like any number of days from my teens or early twenties. There are plenty of other people around, but everything seems typical. I'm by myself reading while I eat. A popular girl a little younger than me sits at the next table. A few other girls join her. I can't help but notice the other girls laugh at her when she pulls out her food. She turns beet red. She pushes her bag of food away and talks with the girls. Something is wrong, clearly, but I can't do anything about it.

I go back to my fries but keep my ears open.

"You have put on a few pounds," one of the girls says in a mocking tone at the girl. I see her face drop to her hands, then she regains her composure.

"Well we'd better get going," a third girl says. They leave her, still laughing.

The girl watches until they are gone, then her shoulders gently rise and fall as she cries silently.

I pick up my own food and walk over to her table. "Can I join you?" I ask. When she looks cautiously at me, I add, "I could use... someone to talk to, ya know?"

"Yeah," she smiles, "I know what you mean. Just don't be a creep."

"I'm Brice."

"Jennifer," she says.

"I don't know about you, but I'm starving." I stuff several fries in my mouth, making her laugh.

"Yeah," she says with a smile and pulls her food back closer to herself.

Jesus is sitting in the front pew by the sacrament table. I am standing a few feet away, facing Him. "Who you are is not a destination you find. There is no treasure map to your true self," He says matter-of-factly. Kind of preachy, actually.

"So it's the journey? What happens to us decides who we become?" I speculate.

"No, the troubles of your life bring out who you have been since before time. Difficult times don't turn you into gold. That would be alchemy, not refining. To refine gold is to melt the imperfections away."

"But they are tests you put us all through? Then you are a bully on an anthill!"

"I am Love; Love does not hurt," He says. "I'm not a bully. The pain in your life enters through sin, sometimes you, usually someone else's. It's too complicated to pinpoint every causation. No, it doesn't mean you deserve any of it. I... I am the healing after the pain, not the cause of the suffering."

"So you know everything I've ever done." I'm not sure why I say it, but it rings true.

"Yes, and my offer for living water is also true." He smiles and looks at the pitcher of water on the table in front of Him.

When I hesitate, He adds, "You have done more to change hearts than you give yourself credit for, you know."

I look up at Him sheepishly.

"I... I mean, I try. That's all I can do, is try," I mumble.

Jesus smiles.

Chapter 11

"I am a thief, I am a murderer
Walking up this lonely hill
What have I done? No, I don't
remember
No one knows just how I feel
And I know that my time is coming
soon"

Thief by Third Day

CATHERINE

"You want to do something, to feel like you're making progress."

"Yes," I say.

"How about the small stuff, with Theodore," Jesus suggests.

'*Well, it could be worse*,' I think. "Okay."

"Where do we start?" He asks.

"Where *do* we start?" I repeat and sigh. A scene of my apartment appears around us. It must have been early on in our 'relationship.' I resent calling it that, even in my head. That wasn't really what it was. "Initially I thought Theodore was going to be so good for me. At times he wasn't so bad, or so I thought. He really listened

to what I had to say even if he was a little han—
"

"I already know. It's okay."
"I wish you'd stop saying that." I roll my eyes.
"What?"
"'It's okay.' It's not." My voice is barely a whisper now and I can't even look Jesus in the eye. "What he did was not okay. Even the 'little' stuff wasn't 'okay.' I'm not okay. Nothing about anything is okay." My voice continues to rise until I am almost yelling. I feel a little ridiculous at my outburst.
"I won't say that anymore if it bothers you."
I've heard that before so I nod and think, 'yeah right'. I just want to move on already.
"I only mean—I mean I'm here, now. He isn't. I mean you're safe," He says softly.
My expression softens a little, but I still doubt anything will change. It never really does.
I look back at the scene in front of us. We're at my place drinking. It's not much, but Theodore definitely introduced me to some more tempting tastes in alcohol. Even more tempting than the taste was that numbness that came afterward. Even one glass of the right stuff could do the trick and melt away any pain, any annoyance, any sadness, any feelings at all. I stare blankly, not truly focusing my eyes on anything so it's all a blur. That numbness is engulfing me again now. Everything is swallowed up into a void. I am swimming in inky blackness. Do I even exist anymore? Maybe not. I think I hear something but it's hard to tell. There is something pawing at my hand, I think. No, I don't want to go back.

I don't want to feel it anymore; any of it. Good or bad, it doesn't matter; it all hurts in the end. The pawing is more insistent now. Go away. Five more minutes, don't pull me out of this—this. What is this? Suddenly it's not so empty inside me. I'm full—of deep and unending pain. I have so much regret. I am not who I want to be. I never will be. Something warm is rubbing against me. Is it a dog? A cat maybe? I can't remember where I am, who I'm with, or what, I'm not even completely sure who I *am* in this abyss. "Catherine," I hear softly. That's right. That's who I am.

Something warm is pulling me back from the void, but I'm not sure I want to leave. Feeling nothing really isn't so bad. At least it doesn't hurt.

"Catherine."

That's my name again. I have to step back out of the oblivion.

Sounds are the first things that come into focus. It is like someone is playing the piano, but in a distant room with all the doors in between shut tight. It's beautiful but I can't quite catch the tune no matter how hard I focus on it. Focusing on it pulls me further out of myself though; out of the nothingness.

Next, colors explode around me in a blur that slowly comes back into focus. I'm back at the church. I feel something under me, something next to me. I can start to orient myself to this space. Something is pulling at my side, but I don't recognize the feeling. The last of my senses to return is smell and I start to smell bread and flowers on the air.

"I'm here. You're not alone."

I turn to see Him. At first, I am not sure I remember who He is or why I'm here. Suddenly everything comes rushing back to me and hits like a freight train. I suck in a quick, and therefore shallow, breath that does more harm than good. Now I can't seem to breathe right. I am overwhelmed and confused. I want to go back to nothingness rather than face all this chaos. Two things stick out to me, but I struggle to put my finger on them in my confusion. Every time I try to name them in my mind, the thought slips away and is replaced by something loud, bright, and abrasive around me.

"I'm here with you."

There's one. "You didn't say 'it's okay,'" I say.

A warmth rises within me. Even in my own confusion, I don't think I have ever felt so understood; so tenderly cared for. It was only two words, two very common, ordinary words, but getting rid of them was such a relief. I am finally free here, I think; at least a little.

"What"—I don't really want to finish my question. It's probably better to move on, but I ask it anyway. "What was that? That emptiness?"

"You know it well. It's depression. That's why I thought it would be a good place to start to work through your pain."

"It—was that a demon?"

"It's another piece you need to heal when you're ready. That won't be for some time though. It's an old friend that won't come easily."

I look at Jesus, confused. "A friend?" I ask.

"Yeah," He says matter-of-factly, "what else would depression be?" He sees my wide-eyes and adds, "An ill-guided, over-protective friend that lies to you—but is just trying to protect you from people and things that it thinks will hurt you. It keeps protecting you until you are alone with only it. Then nothing can hurt you."

I lean back, pondering His words. "Nothing but myself," I mutter, then add, "I never thought of it that way."

My thoughts wander to all the pain I have caused myself.

"That needs to heal too."

Jesus smiles His knowing smile. "What's the other thing on your mind?"

I hate when He knows these things before I do, but I suppose it's to be expected when He knows *all* things.

BRICE

I can see the popular kids coming my way. Here we go.

But they—they walk right by me.

"They didn't always hurt you with their words or their hands. Sometimes the pain comes from being invisible."

"I never stopped to think about that. I wanted to be invisible, to be left alone, but yeah, being invisible hurts, too," I say. "I knew I wasn't invisible to you. I guess my faith kept me going."

"Most of the time."

I look around for Jesus. Again, I can't seem to find Him.

"Do you want to be healed?" Jesus asks me pointedly, from behind me.

I turn, but my eyes are still adapting to my return to the dimly lit chapel. I am dazed and confused, but I respond, "Yes. Yes of course," hoping I don't fail some test of faith or lose an opportunity suddenly presented to me.

Jesus smiles and looks into my eyes. "Then do it."

"I—what? I can't," I stammer.

"But you can and if you look around, you already are doing it."

I gulp as He says this, but He smiles and sort of nods to me but at my chest. I look down and my tunic looks a little cleaner. I can still see something moving in the shadows out of the corner of my eye.

CATHERINE

I see a little pair of red eyes blinking at me from across the aisle. A head appears from the shadows. I tilt my head and it follows suit.

"You're not so scary, are you?" I crouch down and hold out my hand to beckon it over to me. Not as much as my Hate over in the corner. A moment of doubt sets in first. "It's not going to bite my hand off, is it?"

"No," Jesus replies.

"So I need to tame my demons? This doesn't look that hard."

"You need to accept the parts of yourself you struggle with."

"Like?"

He points to the little monster still inching toward me. "Your rage."

It has now reached me and is purring. "What's not to accept? Once you get over the initial unsettling nature of these things."

"Taming it isn't accepting it."

I am thoroughly confused but don't want to admit it.

"You don't get it, but you will."

I change the subject again.

"He had no right," I say under my breath. The demon suddenly rolls over and growls, looking around suspiciously. Maybe there is something to what He said about them protecting me. I wonder if that can come in handy…

"There is a little more we need to talk about now."

"Oh?" I ask. "What now?"

"We need to talk about those scars on your arms."

I stiffen. I knew it was coming at some point. Guess it's time to get real.

I am in my bathroom alone. It is eerie to watch myself, especially with a man, even if He is perfect. I fill the bathtub carefully. I look at the bath then at my bare skin before me. It has betrayed me, I think to myself. It makes me out to be perfect, but I'm not. It looks pure, but it's not. There isn't a blemish in sight, but underneath… If only the inside would show through. It only everyone could see what I see, then it wouldn't be so difficult. I wouldn't have to be so perfect.

I get into the hot water and lean back, closing my eyes before tears can escape.

"Can we go?" I squeak out to Jesus, turning away. I hate watching these shameful moments from my life.

"I was here with you," He says, taking my hands in His. "I am—I'm always with you, even in the moments like this."

In the bath, I have stuffed down my tears and I pick up my razor. I turn away from the scene again. I try to swallow, but my throat is dry. 'Can we go?' It is the only thought that keeps repeating in my head.

I knew in my heart I wasn't alone then, yet I can't tolerate sharing this moment now.

"That's enough," Jesus says lovingly. "It's not meant to hurt, but to heal." He hugs me.

"I'm tired. I want to go home," I say.

It is a very different scene when I become aware of my surroundings again. It is my house, the one I first moved into on my own, just around the corner from my favorite bar. I'm alone on the couch and just starting to stir.

"Look, I know it was wrong to do that—to be like that. I"—I start to cry—"I made my amends and all that. You don't need to put me through it all again."

"This isn't a punishment," Jesus says. "There are still amends that need to be made, but this, this is for you. You need to heal."

On the couch, I stir a little more and roll over and off, onto the floor into a clumsy heap of appendages and clothing thrown together.

I turn away in shame.

"I did it to myself. I let this happen," I begin to sob.

Jesus wraps His arm around my shoulder. "It hurt," He says. I laugh, remembering the hangovers and He continues, "And not just in that way." He tries to smile. "It hurts inside. It hurt others, as you know, and it hurt Me."

I look up and feel even more miserable. I never thought of that. My addiction hurt my God.

Back at the church, I am alone again. I panic a little. What if He's left? Maybe my alcoholism really was too much...

I look over and Jesus is again on the ground. This time He is on His hands and knees, His head bowed between His arms. The crown of thorns is still pressed to His brow, not falling off, even with His head down. I reach Him swiftly and drop to a knee. I gingerly reach under His left arm and chest to raise Him. He leans into me as He lifts to His knees and sits back on His heels. He takes a deep, slow breath before speaking.

"I'm beginning to feel weak," He murmurs.

"Can we rest? Do you need to eat? I can grab the bread," I suggest.

He manages to pull His legs out from beneath Himself so He is seating, leaning a little now.

"I can't. Not right now." He bows His head. I sit next to Him and His head slides to my shoulder, carefully so the thorns avoid my skin. He stretches His legs in front of Him. His chest gently rises and falls. Rest it is, then. Anything, anything You need for having to go through this.

BRICE

I lie on my back in my bed, staring at the ceiling. There isn't really anything on my mind, just a void consuming me. My phone beside me buzzes. I look to see a message from a friend, but I don't have the energy to answer him. I go back to staring at a spot on the ceiling of my dorm room.

"So?" I turn to Jesus.

He smiles weakly. "Your friend was just trying to be there for you. A lot of people were."

"I know," I say, "I just…" But I don't really have a response.

We are back at the chapel, but I am so lost in thought I don't notice the skinny demon until it rubs against my leg.

"Argghhh," I yell and pull my leg away.

It whimpers and retreats, but not too far. It blinks four rosy eyes, two at a time.

I look at Jesus, then back at the demon. I look back at Jesus. "What?" is all I ask.

"It's looking for love," He replies.

"Ewww, why? Why would anyone love something as horrid as that?" I ask, disgusted. I think I see a tear in the demon's eyes. I feel some remorse, but I mean, it's a demon, I think meekly.

"Remember, it's a part of you," Jesus says kindly.

"A part of me wants to be loved… okay, that makes sense, but why a demon? What part of me could become that?" I wonder out loud.

"That's lust."

"*What*?" I yell so loud the demon squeaks again and hides feebly behind a chair leg.

I soften my voice so I'm not yelling. "I'm not lustful," I correct Jesus.

He raises one eyebrow as He responds, "There isn't a part of you that would do *anything* to be loved?"

I deflate somewhat. "Not *anything*. *Some* things, maybe even *most* things, but not *any*thing." I'm the one whimpering by the end of my statement. Maybe I'm not as righteous as I thought.

Chapter 12

"She opens her hand to the poor and reaches out her hands to the needy. She is not afraid of snow for her household, for all her household are clothed in scarlet."

Proverbs 31:20-21

CATHERINE

Jesus walks to the back of the cathedral and stops at a picture by the entryway. I make my way over to His side, but I don't see the significance of the picture. It's just a bunch of women huddled together. The picture is about a charity; maybe I didn't give enough to help them. I look at Him for some clue and tears are in His eyes as He gently reaches up to touch a woman's face.

I get a sick feeling in the pit of my stomach that this isn't about *these* women.

BRICE

It takes me a moment to realize I am sitting alone again. I look around and find Jesus standing near the back of the chapel, again looking at something. I step over broken chairs and around a pile of plaster to stand next to Him. I don't see anything of importance as I scan the table in front of Him. I see a paper with a picture, some signup sheets, information on volunteer opportunities, and a prayer pamphlet. I pick up the prayer pamphlet and thumb through it casually. Only after I put it down do I see He is still focusing on the same spot. I look at Jesus' face and a deep feeling of guilt starts in my stomach; tears are in His eyes. I follow His gaze to the picture and I look closer. It is a group of women gathered by a river in meager clothes. I'm not sure what connection I am supposed to make, but I am sure it has to do with the sour feeling rising in my throat.

CATHERINE

The church changes around me. It's not the empty church that's falling apart back in purgatory. The pews are scattered with people, though they aren't full. It could be any Sunday from the past twenty years. My heart sinks when I see I am sitting with the other musicians. It wasn't just any Sunday, it was the day I lost hope.

I'm not sure what to say but I feel like I need to say something. I open my mouth, but He beats me to it.

"You stopped singing after today. I miss your voice."

"Really? That's what you're concerned about? I didn't keep singing? What can I say? I didn't feel like rejoicing after"—my voice breaks as tears well in my eyes.

Jesus wraps his arm around my shoulder. "Singing isn't just about rejoicing. Some of the most beautiful songs are lamentations."

Through my tears, I still manage to squeak, "You abandoned me. That's why I stopped singing. You weren't here for me and I—I lost her." I can't look up at him though I can tell he is trying to make eye contact. "I don't know how you could let that happen. Why? Why let me suffer like that? Take away someone's life before it even started."

"I didn't abandon you, your pain is my pain." He gently twists his arm to expose the open wounds on his wrists. "Neither of you deserved this pain."

"It wasn't my fault."

"I didn't say it was."

"Then why didn't You stop it? I was right there!" I point. "I was in Your house for God's sake!" I pause for a second at the irony of what I just said, but I am not to be deterred. "I did everything right. I followed the rules. I was living for you. I was singing in the damn choir! And still, you punished me. You took her from me before I could even hold her. All I got to experience of her was an ultrasound with her heartbeat, but just days later she was gone. And I had to—she was gone forever. How could you create something, some*one*, then not even give her a chance?"

I look over at my past self, and—it's happening. Though no one else notices, I know what to look for, blood drips down my leg, barely visible between my knee and my boots.

"The day you lost hope."

"*You abandoned me*!" I screamed. "And her. Of course I lost hope. One day hearing the heartbeat and hearing it'll be okay, it's fine, it's not *that* much bleeding, it happens. Then to have that—that empty feeling. I was supposed to—I wasn't supposed to feel relieved. But the exhaustion was over. I knew it was coming and it did. But still, to have her ripped away as a part of your *divine plan*!" I snap back at him. As I snap, so does part of the ceiling. Two beams fall and land a few pews away, startling me. I hadn't even noticed we were back in purgatory.

"That wasn't our plan. Death never is," Jesus says calmly, "but I am always here for you when you face it. I try to fill the emptiness of your loss. If you let me. I am with everyone when they die, and everyone they leave behind."

I sit solemnly. "Nothing helps with a loss like this. I never ever got to hold her. And then she was just… gone."

After a pause I continue, though my voice is shaking, "Others don't feel the loss like that. If they don't see it, they don't feel it. That little one that was inside me. I felt her. But to everyone else, it's like she never really existed. But she did. I—I heard her heartbeat…"

He sits beside me, not saying a word, just being there with His quiet strength. For a long time, He doesn't say anything, and I don't either. We just sit together.

It finally dawns on me. "This is what helps."

He smiles with those twinkling eyes of His. "It's a start," is His only reply.

I sigh with relief. This does feel better.

"Keep going with that. You need to heal, so what else helps?"

"I—there was something that helped but—"

"But what?"

"It"—I have the feeling He already knows what I am about to say and this scares me. What if it isn't okay? In fact, I know it isn't.

"There is nothing you can say to push Me away. 'Where could I go to escape from you? Where could I get away from your presence? If I went up to heaven, you would be there; if I lay down in the world of the dead, you would be there. If I flew away beyond the east of lived in the farthest place in the west, you would be there to lead me, you would be there to help me. I could ask the darkness to hid me or the light around me to turn into night, but even darkness is not dark for you, and the night is as bright as the day,'" He says comfortingly.

"Psalm 139—part of it. I…" I'm still not sure.

"All *good* things are from God."

"All?"

He nods reassuringly.

"But—it—it wasn't Christian—"

"Neither was I."

We both laugh.

"You have something to say, so say it. It's only about healing here. If it helps heal, use it." He takes my hand.

I take a slow, deep breath. "I—I heard this part of the Qur'an, about—about life." His smile is strengthening my resolve to go on. "From Chapter 23, The Believers: (12-15) 'We created man from an essence of clay, then We placed him as a drop of fluid in a safe place, then We made that drop into a clinging form, and We made that form into a lump of flesh, and We made that lump into bones, and We clothed those bones with flesh, and later We made him into other forms—glory be to God, the best of creators!—then you will die...' It's just—that image of a clinging form and"—tears fill my eyes again—"It's obvious, to me at least, the opposite of that clinging form"—I can't finish my thought out loud.

He finishes it for me, for once, "The opposite is a form that doesn't cling, the loss before it is even finished forming. The opposite is a miscarriage, stillbirth, and the loss of both a child and a mother; a chance to be a mother."

I am in the bathroom looking down and seeing clots and blood in the toilet. No form to it, just a blob, but—I know what it was supposed to become. The very part of me that was supposed to make me a mother has betrayed me. Am I even a woman if I can't bring life? I know better, but I doubt what I am as the emptiness around me threatens to consume me.

I snap back to the present, or I think that is what I should call this. "So the Qur'an is right?"

"Yes."

"And the Bible is right?"

"Yes. 'No truth is profane. In the mouth of a profane man, all truth is sacred.' My brother Scaliger[1] said that," Jesus replies.

"Next you're going to tell me the Book of Mor—um, never mind." I blush. "They can't all be right, can they?"

"God has many faces. You have only seen a few. In fact, everyone sees a slightly different face of God."

"So—I mean that's almost like—like there's more than one God."

"No, all the Divine is one, everlasting, unchanging. It's"—He pauses thoughtfully like He's trying to explain rocket science to an ant. I feel so small and simple-minded. He holds something out in His hand. It looks like a diamond.

He goes on, "God is like a jewel, a many-faceted gem. And"—here He rolls it between His fingers—"you can't see all sides at once."

"But someone else can see that side," I exclaim, looking through the jewel at Him. I am quite proud of myself for catching on already. I look at the light reflecting from the jewel dancing on everything around me.

"Yeah, that's a lot like Him, too. Reflecting His light everywhere."

I smile contently, but then—wasn't I just grieving? It washes over me again along with immense guilt. Now I'm smiling and it feels all wrong.

"Why?" He probes.

"Why what?"

"Why does it feel wrong to be happy again?"

"Because I was just so sad."

144

It feels utterly ridiculous to put into words, but I try. I'm learning if anyone is going to understand, He will.

"If I was really that sad then I can't just flip it off like this. If—if I really miss her, I can't be happy right now!"

"Or, by that logic, ever again."

"Well—"

He smiles like He has some deep insight for me. "You can be happy and sad."

"No, that's"—I stop. Why am I trying to argue with the Son of God? That's probably not going to end well for me.

"You never sang after that day. I felt that loss too, but I also welcomed Hope. You'll see her."

The change in topic was so abrupt, I wasn't sure what He was talking about.

"I'll—what? Who?"

"Hope, your daughter. You really did lose Hope that day."

I pause stunned. I wasn't far enough along to name her, but it made sense. Suddenly it all made sense. "Can I see her?"

"Not yet, like with Jennifer, you still have so much pain to let go."

I go from feeling relieved to heavy again.

"Will this ever end?" I sigh.

"Yes." He gives me a comforting smile. "You have your whole life to work through, but this process only extends as far as your life and your impacts do. It will take time, and then it will end. Like life, too."

I feel even heavier, but He lifts my chin, "We have a lot of good things to talk about too. This isn't a punishment, always remember that." He picks up a songbook and opens it.

I smile through my tears as I join Him in the song.

"Amazing grace…" we sing.

When it is finished, He wraps an arm around my shoulders. I am surprised at how much comfort I get from this. I was never much of a hugger.

"We still need to talk about Hope."

"We definitely still need to talk about—that," I reply and shuffle my feet. Panic washes over me. "Is—did I kill her?" I can't avoid the guilt or the tears suddenly gushing down my cheeks.

"No," He softly replies.

We're back at the church. One of the little monsters scurries out from under a pew, its orange eyes shining and blinking. I look at it but quickly turn away again. It is an unnerving little beast. Out of the corner of my eye, I see it make its way to the table.

"No!" I yell and stomp my foot in its direction.

It yelps and rushes away into the shadows again.

BRICE

I'm back at the church but something seems different. I can't quite place it, but something—something's missing. I was never that good at details though, so I can't figure out what.

Jesus is still standing beside me.

"So that's it?" I ask him.

"For now. Things like this take time. This can be a place to rest and find yourself again."

146

As if I could lose myself. Wait, did I just see something move in the corner? When I look over there's nothing there. Not more demons.

"Um—so what's next?" I say.

"Always the go-getter."

"What can I say? When something needs to be done, I do it."

"That you do. We'll work on that, too."

"Wait—what?" I say, startled. Is there something wrong with doing what needs to be done? But in a flash, everything changes.

We're at the park with my kids. It seems like a nice enough memory. I can't think of anything painful that happened.

"It's not your pain we're here to heal."

"But I thought—did—did I—hurt someone here?"

I'm not that kind of guy, he has to believe that.

"Not directly, you could say," He says coyly.

"I'm so confused."

"Watch and listen."

I look at myself with my head down, engrossed in playing with my own three children. Devin is teetering along behind Jax, who is doting on Peia. Jax always was looking out for his little sister. Jax, the oldest, always the helper. I smile a bittersweet smile.

"See you soon," I whisper to him.

That isn't what this is about though? What am I missing?

"Mommy, I need help," I hear a little girl on the other side of the playground say.

"I would like you to try to do it by yourself," someone not too far away says.

"I can help her," someone else chimes in.

"That isn't necessary, she can do it herself," the mom says.

"No problem at all," the other woman says and scoops up the child. To the child, she says, "Clearly your mom is *very* busy over there."

"I just like her to try things herself. Gracie, let's just go," the mom sighs, clearly exhausted.

"Well that's uncalled for!" the other woman huffs away.

I turn to Jesus. "I'm still confused. I think I know her, but I don't see how I—what I—did wrong. It wasn't my business."

"It's what you didn't do," Jesus points out to me. I am closer now and I clearly heard the conversation, but I was doing the thing I do when I try to be invisible and go unnoticed rather than get involved. I turn back to my kids and smile as Jax gently picks up Peia and helps her over the step she's struggling to climb.

"Oh, so I was supposed to stand up for her?"

Tears are quietly streaming down the woman's face, but are barely noticeable. Clearly, she is having a rough time.

"She needed some compassion at that moment. She was going through far more than you realize."

A crow-like bird hops out of a dark doorway. Its feathers glisten in the candlelight. A medium-sized fan tail spreads behind it and it steps toward me. I don't know what it is, but I know enough to not trust it. I do admit it is strikingly beautiful. It turns its head slightly. It blinks, but I shudder a little seeing the eyelids move horizontally then vertical. The eyes of the creature are hypnotic amethysts. The purple is calming and alarming at the same time. I close my eyes to avoid the creature's gaze.

When I open my eyes, I am sitting in a pew with Jesus beside me. His eyes are closed and He looks like He is concentrating. I sit quietly, not wanting to disturb Him, but I soon grow bored and impatient.

What is He doing? Why? Is He sleeping? No, that isn't it. I shuffle my feet in front of me, then finally I get the courage to tap His shoulder. I intend to clear my throat also to get His attention, but I gasp instead as a power surges through me.

Jesus opens His eyes with a pained expression for a moment.

"I didn't mean to—I'm sorry," I babble.

He takes a deep breath in and out. "It's okay," He says.

I look down sheepishly, wishing I was anywhere else.

Chapter 13

"Through many dangers, toils and snares
We have already come.
T'was grace that brought us safe thus far
And grace will lead us home"

Amazing Grace

CATHERINE

I put down the glass and for a moment, just the briefest moment, I see my reflection there. Fitting, since I am as empty as it is.

It's hard to watch my drunken despair.

"I know... I know it was wrong." I turn away, but Jesus sits on the couch next to the younger me. Meekly, I look back at Him. He isn't paying attention to me, not the current me anyway. I'm sitting on my couch drinking away my pain. Jesus reaches out to hold my hand. He just misses as I move it to raise the glass to take a drink. He tries again, this time reaching for my cheek, but I lean forward, pour the bottle, and fill the glass I just emptied. He tries to wrap His arm around my shoulder, but I sigh and sag forward.

He leans over to me, but I rise and walk to the kitchen looking for another bottle.

"I'm sorry—I didn't know—I know there's no excuse for how I acted," I say, watching myself in the kitchen. "It's no wonder you gave up on me and waited for me to come back to you."

"I never gave up on you. I never will." He stands and walks over to the counter I'm leaning against. He wraps His arms around me as I slump over my glass. I sigh and place my head against His chest. For a moment everything is perfect. It's perfect until I grab my glass again and put it in the sink, frustrated at its emptiness. I leave the kitchen and stumble to my bathroom. My movement knocks Jesus over and He falls to the ground.

I look over at Jesus and He says, "I'll never give up on you, Catherine."

BRICE

I'm in a memory again, or back in time. I'm still trying to make sense of these parts of my life.

I'm walking along a road at night. I really did leave for the library, but somehow I end up in a different direction. I walk to the bridge overlooking the interstate. I don't know if I remember how I got here, but here I am. I step up to the rail and watch as cars, trucks, semis; vehicles of all different shapes and sizes zoom below. '*It wouldn't take that much,*' I think to myself as a lone tear starts to well in my eye.

I don't know exactly where this deep darkness inside of me is coming from, but it is all-consuming and intoxicating. It blots out Bryan. It blots out my mother's favoritism. It even blots out my father's disappointment. It absorbs my failures and wipes out my loneliness. Without these, I am left with a deep emptiness and the traffic passing below.

The lights are hypnotic as they zoom past. I am a moth drawn to their flame. Going to the light means I don't have to go back home again. Going to the light means I don't have to go back to school again. Going to the light means I don't have to go back to anything. I can be consumed by the darkness. I won't have to feel angry or disappointed or sad or lonely ever again. I won't have to feel anything again.

"You okay?" someone behind me asks.

I stiffen. "Fine," I lie, but I stay where I am. I won't let her see me cry. That's when I see Jesus is standing next to me on the very edge of the overpass.

"I know it's tempting sometimes," the voice says, next to me now, "but it won't really help."

"I—I don't know what you're talking about," I reply.

"So you do have a tough guy side," she laughs, but not in a mean way. I can't help but crack a smile. I think it's a little less dark suddenly. Finally, I turn to face her. I'm still not quite sure how much I can trust her. But as I watch, Jesus is right there beside me on the bridge.

"I feel it too... sometimes." There is a deep sadness in her voice that makes her more believable, then she adds, "It's okay that it's not okay, if that makes any sense."

152

"I know what you mean actually," I laugh, then the darkness strikes again. "What if it's never okay again?"

"It's—I mean there's still a reason to stick around. The future doesn't make up for the present. I know what you mean, but—you don't need to stick around because it might get better. It also might get worse—no, hear me out! You can't rely on what might happen. You don't have to make it better or save the world or something. You don't have to do anything to earn the right to stick around. You are needed somewhere, by someone—you'll probably never know who or when or why. Trust me, I never seem to feel that helpful and it never feels like it's enough of a difference to mean anything. So why stick it out? But I am sure, someone, somewhere, sometime needs you, just the way you are."

She kind of nudges my arm and I smile a little. I still feel so overwhelmed.

"I'm—I'm not sure I'm strong enough"—my voice cracks and I can't even finish my thought.

"Me too," she says with a trembling voice, "but I'm going to keep trying."

I let out a deep slow breath. "Yeah I"—I feel a weight lifting off my shoulders. Jesus tries to put an arm around my shoulder, but I finally step down. I look at my feet as He joins me and embraces me, crying.

"That's better," Catherine says and walks away. "I don't even really remember that—I mean I know I had… dark times—but I didn't… really I didn't mean it…"

CATHERINE

I slump to the floor of my old house. I don't want to face this, but I know I have to. It's just so… shameful. I stumble off the couch and manage to drag myself into the bathroom. After a bit, I stumble into the kitchen to find something to help with my hangover. I am surprised when I find a protein bar and a note on the counter. I know I didn't leave that there.

I wouldn't know, but I've heard protein helps hangovers. If you need help getting sober, or finding God, you can reach out to me—Brice.

"What?" I crumble the note and toss it in the trash, missing it barely. "When was he…" Then I remember he helped me home last night.

"I guess he was trying to help. Could have been worse, at least he didn't leave his missionary stuff. Probably would have tried to baptize me when I was blacked out." I shrug and open the protein bar, but have to run to the trash can at the smell of it. I edge around the counter, away from the vomit-inducing gift to the fridge. I pull out some eggs and start my real hangover cure. On the way I pick up the crumpled note and put it back on the counter.

The dead me is still sitting on the floor in the living room, but I have a clear view of everything. I'm not sure why I'm here, but I question if it is worth it to ask.

As I go about my business in the kitchen, something seems to change. There is a difference in the air, but I can't name it.

"Sober," my younger self whispers at the stove. "Maybe it is time to change things around."

I turn away from my younger self and to Jesus to say, "But I didn't, not then. I failed several times and—"

Jesus reaches down a hand to help me to my feet. I am too miserable to take it, but He nudges me insistently. I take it and rise but avoid His gaze.

"But today was the start of that difficult journey. Yes, you struggled, but today you started to get sober."

It took twenty-one days though. Twenty-one days before I show up at a meeting. I have to find one, I tell myself. I need to go someplace I'm comfortable, so not the first one I find. It has to work with my schedule, so that crosses other meetings off my list. After eighteen days, I sit and look at my remaining list, but... without another excuse, I put the list away. As I walk away, I spy the note Brice left me. I walk back and pull the list out again and circle a meeting three days from now.

I walk into the community center and nervously look at the list of rooms and meetings. Maybe I should go to Beginning Pottery instead? Or maybe Taxes Made Easy? No, I need to get sober, I need to go to... room 109, down the hall around the corner past all those other classrooms. Doubtful, I start my trek through the building. I double back when I take a wrong turn, but finally I reach room 109. I take a deep breath and walk in. Might as well just rip off the band-aid already.

I sit in the only available chair in the circle of folding chairs. Everyone smiles at me. I awkwardly smile back.

"Welcome," the man to my right says.

Even though I haven't been here before, I've heard about it, so I begin, "Hi, my name is Catherine and I'm an alcoholic."

"Hi, Catherine."

Back at the cathedral, I can't find Jesus. Is He ever going to just be where I expect Him to be? Or do I always have to guess?

This time I find Jesus flat on the ground, face down. He is slightly dusted with plaster so I can see the subtle rise and fall of His breathe as the powder lifts in the air ever so slightly and settles again. At least He is alive.

I sit down next to Him.

"Can you get up again?" My voice is shaky and cracks a little. Tears fill my eyes as I am overcome with a deep sadness.

"I"—His voice cracks too, but He rises a little. I put my left arm under His chest and press up just a little. Soon He is up on all fours again. From there, I help Him to sit and lean against the wall. When I feel like He isn't going to fall over again, I jog to the table to grab a piece of bread. I return to His side and break off a piece. He smiles, but says, "Not yet," and sighs.

"This takes a lot out of You, to help people work through their life."

"This is my work, my life."

I feel a deep sadness. "You do this over and over again—forever."

"Yes."

"I—don't you"—I pause trying to think of the right words—"want more? I mean you have to fix everyone?"

He smiles. "You do the work. I just show the way."

"But—you're—what you go through… this… it's taking so much out of you."

"My life. But as I said, 'there is no greater love than to lay down one's life for a friend.'"

I reach over and He takes my hand.

"Then I am glad you are my friend," I say and sit back against the wall next to Him.

He smiles in return.

I am still looking at Jesus when, out of the corner of my eye, a spindly-legged, pink-eyed creature emerges. It looks like a large spider, but taller and thinner. It moves in a cartoonish, slinky way. I take a second look and stifle a laugh; it has long eyelashes. It might as well *be* a cartoon spider. It stops several feet away and blinks its four rosy eyes at me in what I can only describe as 'puppy dog' eyes.

"What does it want?" I ask Jesus.

"What does anything want?" When I struggle to find a response, He continues, "to be loved. Lust always starts that way somewhere deep down, a need to be loved to some degree."

I don't know if I agree about lust, in general, but I can see how this animal is very clearly looking for affection.

BRICE

Jesus is holding a book in His hands as He sits next to me. He waits for me to adjust to my new surrounding then He says, "It was a simple message and yet you people can turn it into a whole book!"

I try to catch up, but I am thoroughly confused and it shows.

"I think some people call them the Beatitudes." I am still confused, so He continues, "Or the Sermon on the Mount?"

"Oh yeah, happy are those that…"

"Yeah, yeah."

"I like those," I say sheepishly.

"Yeah, a list of do this, don't do that. Not that difficult," He lectures.

"Well, I think people struggle with whether or not we're doing it right."

Jesus smiles. "Gotta start somewhere."

"Is—is there anything I can do?" I manage to squeak out pathetically.

He smiles. "Can't you see what I am doing for you?"

I sit by the steps with my head down. Something slowly moves into the top of my field of vision. I don't want to deal with this right now. I close my eyes and rub my temples. I open my eyes again and the demon has moved an inch or so forward and is looking at me lazily.

"Not right now," I say to it.

It closes its one large eye and appears to take a nap.

Chapter 14

"How quickly we reject ourselves,
blinded by the call.
We resign to live in fear of love, of self,
of all.
This is not the will of God
For the chosen must be free.
We are taken by the love of Christ to
live eternally

Like the bread, we are taken.
Like the Christ, we are blessed.
On this altar we are broken,
giv'n as food that all might live,
giv'n as food that all might live.

Broken like the bread of life,
we often flee from pain.
We resign to live our lives,
not knowing death's true gain.
This is not the will of God,
for in dying we will live.
The cross, a sign of victory
and the healing it will give.

Like the Bread Tom Booth

CATHERINE

We're at Theodore's apartment again. It's Halloween so there are a few decorations around. Tears are already filling my eyes.

"Do I have to relive this again? I…"

"You already relive it far too often, my child," He says. "I do not intend for it to hurt you anymore."

We are back at the church suddenly. Relief washes over me, followed by dread.

"But if I don't face it now, I'll just have to later right?"

"Let's talk instead. Words have a lot of power." Jesus pauses, then continues, "You need to let go of all your burdens, the ones given to you as well as the ones you picked up yourself." Jesus looks into my eyes.

I look down, but reply, "You said I needed to let go of my sins." Looking up again, my voice rising in anger, I continue, "I didn't do anything wrong." I began to shake from my anger, meeting his compassion with my fire. "Him, *he* is the one you need to talk to. He needs to atone for this."

The fire on the candles blazed with all my fury, endangering any nearby objects with their inferno. The room rumbles all around.

Softly, lovingly, he replies, "He will, I will meet him, just as I am meeting you, and he will face everything that he has done and that was done to him as well." He looks directly at me and continues, "I am not here to talk about him right now, I am talking about you. You need to let go of your anger; there is no place for it in the kingdom. To heal your pain, you must release these burdens."

"So *he'll* have to face this? I hope he goes to hell for what he did."

Cracks form in one of the adjacent walls, causing a few pieces of plaster to fall to the floor.

"You don't mean that."

"Oh yes, I do!"

The cracks spread at a deafening pace that causes me to rethink my fury, but only for a moment.

"Then you see why you and I need to talk about this?" Always my anger is met with compassion. Is there anything I could do to anger Him in return? I turn away.

"So you can change my mind into forgiving him?" I say with contempt.

"So you can let go," Jesus gently replies.

"But he'll... he'll pay for it, right? There is justice here, even if there isn't always justice on Earth? That's the point of this, isn't it? The good ones go to heaven and the bad go to hell." I say it as more of a statement than a question, though my voice does waver a little. Tears are threatening to spill out of my eyes. The candles flicker and a few are in danger of going out.

"Depends on what you mean by hell. It's not what most people think. It's not fire and brimstone or demons. You all have your own demons inside of you, tearing you apart bit by bit. This place isn't about punishment but about accepting your demons. You create your own hell by holding on to your pain. Let go." He looks up, his eyes piercing right through me. "Are you ready to let go of what he did to you?"

"But if I'm not angry, then how do I protect myself?" I say, quivering, but I realize how ridiculous this sounds, so I add, "He doesn't deserve my forgiveness. If I don't forgive him, then... what's that line in the Bible, 'what I bind on earth, you bind in heaven' or something? Then he will be punished."

"Right now, the only person I see you punishing is yourself." His words sting as if he slapped me in the face. "It is not easy to put down the burdens you carry, but that's why we're here. I am here with you, for as long as it takes. What is under your anger?"

"Wh-what?"

"Why are you angry?"

After a pause, I answer, "He hurt me."

"Pain is what's under your anger. You don't want to relive your pain, you swore you would never be a victim again. Your anger keeps you in your pain, it keeps you from healing. So you are hurting yourself to keep him or anyone else from hurting you. Right now, there is no one left to hurt you but you. It's time to let go."

I can't hold back the tears anymore. They trickle down my face, first one, then two. Soon they are streaming down my cheeks onto my tunic. Sniveling now and then, the tears keep pouring out of me. Then I am sobbing uncontrollably. I have held this flood back for so long. I can't be the victim, but now it pours out full force. I am not sure when he moved, but Jesus is now embracing me. At first, I resist, but only for a moment. I collapse into His embrace, welcoming His warmth, His comfort. For the first time in years, I don't have to think about any 'what if's' and can relax into a man's embrace without fear. Even that moment's hesitation makes my heart sink. Am I really this damaged? I don't know how long I cry. It may be hours, or here in purgatory, it could be years, but the tears finally subside. My tunic again is no longer white but stained with my tears, spots, and streams of off-white coloring and dirt now make it look more like an old tattered rag. I do not look forward to what it will take this time to walk away clean. The other times were uncomfortable enough. This will be outright painful.

"Are you ready?"

I suck in a long breath, steeling my resolve. I have come this far, I can face this too.

"Yes," I whisper.

"What have you always wanted to say to him?"

"What?" I say. Jesus never ceases to surprise me in this ordeal.

"If Theodore was here right now, if he could hear you, *but,*"—He puts a hand up for emphasis—"you don't have to worry about how he would respond what would you say?"

"He can't respond? So I wouldn't have to worry about his mind games?"

Jesus nods.

I sigh. "Oh, where to start?"

After a pause, I continue, "If only words could hurt him as much as he hurt me."

"Words can hurt and they can heal."

Suddenly there is an apparition of him, my ex. I can tell he isn't really there: he doesn't move and has a kind of shimmery, translucent quality. But it is definitely him. I will never forget his face. I suck in a long, slow breath. "I would tell him he hurt me. In ways he'll never understand. It wasn't just my body. He messed up my mind. He did something to my soul. People want to see me get better but it's because they don't see the real damage he did. They don't want to look at it."

I look at the apparition and the words boil out of me, "You hurt me. You will never understand how much. I could never let you see how much." My voice shakes a little, but I continue, "So many times I have wanted you to hurt as much as I did. I have to look over my shoulder. I have to always be careful. It's hard to trust anyone. Sometimes I get scared when I know I shouldn't. And it's all because of *you*." I ball my fists, digging my nails into my palms, "I didn't deserve this pain. I never hurt you. Why would you hurt someone so much? How could you be so *selfish*? That's all that rape is, selfishness. You lost control and you used your power to take from me, take my power but also to take *so much more*." Tears well in my eyes again. "I have tried to put myself back together, but I don't think I have all the pieces anymore."

The ceiling shakes, dust falls from the rafters, the candles rattle, and a pew falls backward. The whole building feels as if it is being torn apart. I am being torn apart.

"I can help with that." Jesus squeezes my shoulder, startling me. I have forgotten He is there.

"I... I don't want to be angry anymore," I weep.

"I can help with that too." Jesus smiles slightly.

The shaking stops. I can see something different about the walls again. It almost looks like water. Like... like the walls are crying along with me.

"I..." I hesitate, but continue softly, "I would tell him, 'I just want you to acknowledge you hurt me. Take responsibility. Say you're sorry. *Be* sorry. Say that you could never say or do anything to make up for what you took from me. I want you to be sorry, not because you have to be punished or are afraid. I can't, I won't misuse power the way you do. I want you to be sorry because you see my pain; because you see *me*. Because I am a person worth seeing, not garbage... *I'm not garbage!*'"

"No, you are not garbage. You are precious, my child." Jesus holds me for a long time again. I notice His hands, the open wounds, they... they are bleeding again.

After a while, He asks, "Do you still feel angry?"

I take a long slow breath before responding. "No. But I can't change the past. It made me who I am... stronger, a survivor." I stiffen and I can feel the room harden around me. Cracked though the walls are, they will not show their weakness.

"Is that really all you are? What's happened to you? You are a child of God. You are my beloved. You were wonderfully and fearfully made. You are so much more than anything that happened to you. You can let go of this. You must let go of this." There's a slight desperation in His voice. Is He afraid of me? Or for me?

"But I need to protect myself to keep from getting hurt again…" Almost as soon as I say this, I laugh, who would I need to protect myself from now? He tilts His chin down, the left side of His mouth is curling up, His eyes are sparkling. Yep, He is definitely reading my thoughts.

He answers in a whisper this time, "Are you ready to let go of what he did to you?"

Tears stream down my cheeks, my lips quiver, and my voice cracks as I try it. "I need to know he'll pay for what he did to me. I need to know there will be justice."

The room begins to tremble again.

He starts to speak.

"*He needs to pay*!" I scream and shoot up, shaking all over. Finally, at the peak of my rage, the beautifully crafted stained-glass windows shatter all around, their rainbows crashing in every direction. The red-eyed demon is by my side ready to pounce. I gasp, aghast at the agony I caused this time. "He needs to pay for what he did to me," I whisper.

I don't notice Jesus getting up until His arms are already around me. I collapse into Him and we slide to the floor in a tangled embrace. I feel like a child again in those protective arms. "He needs to pay," I whisper.

"He is not your concern anymore. You let go of your anger, remember? This is about you and me now." He lifts my chin so I have to meet His gaze. "No one will ever hurt you again." His voice is quivering now. He wipes my tears. "Can you let go of what he did to you?"

No more words come from me, but none are needed. I look down and my garment is a brilliant white again. Before my eyes, the shards of glass rise and spin in whirlwinds of light and color. Something is happening to the walls too, but it is difficult to make it out in all the commotion with the glass. New, even more, spectacular designs form from the shards. The previous depictions of saints and biblical stories are replaced with mosaics of the shards. The largest one is an intricate and beautiful heart. The beauty that comes from my destruction causes more tears to well in my eyes. I am overwhelmed with joy.

BRICE

I don't want to follow the younger me, but I know I can't avoid it. It's why I'm here. No more running away.

Jesus puts His hand on my shoulder. "Do not be afraid, I am with you."

I nod. Slowly I make my way up the stairs, through the door, and into the lion's den. I already hear the yelling as I turn into the empty hallway. Pictures rattle on the walls as I carefully place each foot where the floorboards don't squeak. It dawns on me how ridiculously careful and quiet I am being. It's a memory. They can't hear me, no one can see me, yet I still flinch when I hear Bryan's fist slam on the table. My older brother always had a temper. I don't know why my parents tolerated him, let alone held him up as their ideal, perfect child.

"You're not even my real mother!" Bryan yells.

The words sting me even now. How could he say that to her? My parents taught me we were a family, period. Adoption and biological were words others used to describe us.

My mom's stern façade cracks and she cries.

"I don't even remember why they're fighting," I say to my Companion, my Protector, my Rock in times like this.

"That isn't the point," He responds.

"I know," is all I can muster back.

"Stop acting like such a jerk," the 14-year-old me says in a vain attempt to defend my mother.

Bryan's rage turns on me and is swift and daunting as he grabs me at the base of my neck. His grip pinches slightly as he drags me roughly across the room. He only lets go when he throws my face down at the top of the staircase. His hand still on the back of my neck, I can feel his breath just above his hand. In an eerily calm voice, he says, "Call me a jerk again and I'll throw you down those stairs." He lets go and walks out of the room.

My mom walks over, doesn't offer to help me up, but towering over me, says, "You shouldn't provoke him like that," and walks away again.

The younger me gets up and storms off to my room. "Last time I ever stand up for her," I say to myself.

I crumple to the floor at the foot of my bed. I look next to me, but Jesus isn't there. He bends down and holds the teenage heap that has burst into tears.

I turn away as tears stream down my now slightly wrinkled cheeks. I flinch as Jesus again puts a hand on my shoulder. He doesn't pull away though and instead draws me into a full embrace.

CATHERINE

We're in a very different part of my life.

"Now what?" I snap.

"Just watch," Jesus says.

I'm brushing my teeth. Tim comes up behind me and wraps his arms around me.

The dead me softens a little at the happy memory, but I am unsure of Jesus' motives, which makes me wary.

The younger me puts my toothbrush down and I turn to face Tim as he pulls me close. His breath tickles my neck, making me giggle. I can't help but smile thinking about Tim, but an ache in my chest soon follows. I miss him. Meanwhile, Tim's tenderness is still playful and endearing.

"I can't help myself," he teases.

Both versions of myself stop at his words. It's not his fault. He doesn't know who else used to say that.

"What?" the younger me manages to mutter.

Tim still smiling, explains, "You know I can't help"—he kisses my neck again—"but love you." Then he adds, "Sweet something, sweet something, sweet something," into my ear.

"What?" I'm giggling now.

"You deserve somethings, not nothings," he croons, "so I am whispering sweet somethings to you."

I am standing rather close to them... us... I reach my hand out and touch Tim's cheek. I can't help it; I miss him so much. He smiles and leans into my hand. I pull my hand away shocked. He is still smiling and touches his cheek where my hand was.

The younger me raises my chin a little and he kisses deeply. I melt further into his embrace.

The dead me turns away. "Why are we here?" I grumble.

"You don't see it? It's right there," Jesus points back to the happy couple.

I do not turn. I wish He would turn away.

"Am I making you uncomfortable?"

"Yes."

"Are you ashamed of your love of Tim?"

"No," I replied. "There are just some things... that are... private."

"I understand." He sighs deeply. I hate it when He does that. He continues, "It wasn't always that way. It isn't that way here. It can't be."

My face scrunches. "I'm not sure I understand."

Jesus smiles. "There is no room for shame here. Only love."

"Okay, I get it," I mumble.

"I don't think you do though, Catherine." He looks deeply into my eyes. "It's more than that. Sometimes two broken people, they... they just fit together. Love... love heals."

I think about Tim's embrace, about his sweet somethings, and smile. "Yes, yes it does."

We are back at the cathedral when out of the corner of my eye, I think I see something move in a shadow sending chills down my spine.

"But why? Why do you let bad things happen? Was I not being good enough?"

"Everyone puts too much power behind such a little word. Why this? Why that? Why me? Why now? Why not? You make up fanciful equations of being worthy enough to avoid some suffering and why others slip through. You feel blessed it isn't worse, and give me credit for making your life easy, then curse me when it's not. You ask for a different life on a regular basis, but rarely for the strength to live your own life with dignity and grace. Life isn't about why. It's about how. How am I going to compose myself? How am I going to be transformed by it? Resurrected by it?"

"Wait, didn't you ask God to take away your pain in the garden?"

"Ho ho, touché." He claps my back. "Touché, but what was it I said on the cross? In the thick of it?"

"Forgive them, for they know not what they do," we say together.

"Facing great struggles is either harder or easier when you know you face it tomorrow," He says solemnly. "You don't always have time for such theories when the moment comes."

"You need to learn to forgive before you face that challenge alone."

"Alone? You're leaving me?" I can't help my voice rising.

"Not yet." He smiles, but it is fragile, with pain veiled behind it. "The story isn't over," He says kindly.

I am hurt, but clearly, He is, too. So I drop the subject.

Something is moving to my right… I think. I walk a little closer and peer around a pew to see a cat-sized lump of black that might be moving. It swivels its head to face me with one large blue eye blinking slowly. It yawns and lays its head down again.

"I'm not sure if that's a demon or a giant dust bunny," I laugh.

The blue eye opens again and looks at me.

"So what is it—oh! I know, it's sloth isn't it," I chuckle. "Well, that makes sense."

It yawns again, smacking its lips.

Turning to find Jesus, I cannot believe my eyes. Jesus is standing by the altar, shoulders hunched, head hanging. His tunic, His blood-stained robe, and even His tattered sandals are all missing. He stands there naked and broken. I avert my eyes. I want to offer help, I am ashamed to come near Him in such a state. A movement draws my attention back to His face. Even through His pain-stricken expression, He smiles at me. Something inside me suddenly doesn't feel as broken anymore.

BRICE

I've been in my room for about an hour waiting until things quiet down again. I peek out my door. Mom's in the kitchen. There's no sign of Bryan. Do I take the risk?

"Dinner's ready," Mom yells. I don't have a choice. I slink out, avoiding the squeaky floorboards. Relief washes over me when I see both of my parents in the kitchen and Bryan's nowhere in sight.

I sit down at the table. My mom's not exactly a good cook. The majority of her meals come from a box. My mom hands me a plate of stovetop rice as she chatters away to my dad. It's hard to believe this is the same place, the same woman who stood there an hour ago, but then again, that's my family.

We are at the church again.

Something swoops overhead, brushing right by me. I cover myself protectively, but I think it has passed. I can see amber eyes in the darkness. I wish I wasn't alone with these monsters.

I look for my Companion. I walk up the main aisle of the crumbling chapel. I am surprised and a little terrified when I see Jesus; not of Him, but I am terrified by the hole in the ground He is sitting next to. I step forward. What is underneath this ethereal chapel? I gulp at the thought but keep going. It is part of the process, I think. Whatever it is, it's always part of the process. Jesus reaches into the hole and pulls out…

A rock. It is smooth, although not rounded, more of a flat, rectangular shape. It is a dark, greyish-blackish color. Jesus sets it down next to the hole.

"It's there if you're ready to throw it," He says.

Bile rises in my throat. I have. I have thrown stones my whole life. It's time to be more understanding instead.

I turn and notice a difference. He rises to His feet. His clothes are tattered, torn to shreds. He stands there looking broken. I look around for some sort of clothing, any cloth maybe, but there is nothing of any good around. I keep my eyes down as I walk forward. I hesitate at the steps, but only for a moment before ascending as I quickly whip my tunic over my head. I hand it to Jesus. He smiles but it seems difficult for Him to move. I gently raise the shirt over His head and help His arms through the sleeves. He places a hand on my right shoulder and lays His head on my left, sighing deeply.

"The time draws near."

My stomach turns with pity and remorse. There must be a different way, yet I know there isn't.

Chapter 15

"And when I think of God,
His Son not sparing
Sent Him to die,
I scarce can take it in
That on the Cross,
my burden gladly bearing
He bled and died
to take away my sin"

How Great Thou Art

CATHERINE

"Stop and listen to your feelings. That is how We talk to you."

"Now that people are so closed off to you? We don't hear you anymore, but you still come through in—in—in a primal kind of way?"

"No. This is always how We have spoken to the prophets. We are Love. Love is emotion. All other emotions are connected to it in one way or another. It's true you're not as connected to your emotions anymore."

He waits for me to process this.

"But we all have emotions," I laugh. "You sound as though you are saying we are all prophets."

"That's exactly what I am saying."

BRICE

I'm sitting at a restaurant table eating. I wrack my brain to remember this day, but I simply don't, let alone what I did or didn't do.

I'm alone, but it looks like I'm looking for someone.

A woman walks by in a short skirt. I look down at the menu, then at my watch; anywhere but at her.

A man walks up to her.

"Get lost," she tells him.

"But baby," he whines. "Just come over tonight."

"Teddy, no," she snaps.

"Whatever," he stomps off.

"What are you looking at?" She turns her anger on me.

"Nothing." I shrug and look down.

I turn to Jesus. "So what, I didn't stand up for her? Didn't help her some way?"

"You judged her." My heart sinks. '*I did*,' I think miserably. As I look at her now, I see an edge of pain around her tough exterior.

"She… she could make things easier on herself," I say meekly, but I know it's just an excuse.

"Exactly," Jesus says, "throwing stones at the one hurting is just an excuse."

CATHERINE

I'm at a non-denominational church event with a friend. It's all about our shared love of Jesus. I'm not sure what's so important about this night. It actually seems a little arrogant for Jesus to be here worshiping Himself.

He looks at me. "I'm not here for my own glory," He says crossly, then more seriously, He asks, "Don't you remember when this was?"

"November, I think," I say. "It wasn't all that important even then."

"November first," He says.

Right after Halloween. I hadn't made that connection.

"God is good!" the next speaker bellows from the stage. "What's that? I said *God is good*!" The last time he says it is deafening.

The crowd erupts in response.

"That's better," the speaker replies enthusiastically. "Now, I have a topic the secular world doesn't want me to talk to you about. I've got news the media won't report to you. I have a message—a message straight from God himself. Are you ready for it?"

The crowd erupts boisterously again.

"The message I have for you is…"—he drops his voice for dramatic effect leaving us on the edge of our seats—"about chastity. That's right sex isn't all it's made out to be—before marriage, that is."

My mouth goes dry as I watch the younger me sink in my pew, wishing I could be invisible.

"I"—but my voice cracks. I'm not sure what to say anyway. My stomach turns as I feel that sting again.

Jesus gently puts His hand on my shoulder. "I came to heal, not to judge." He turns His gaze toward the stage, "He doesn't mean to judge either. He's trying." He looks around now. "They all are—trying that is." He looks at me again, "It isn't meant to hurt like this."

"It wasn't my fault," I whisper.

"I know," Jesus says.

"And all this"—I wave my arm at the crowd—"it was all… all about one thing. One way to be right. There's no room for—for someone like me." I look down, ashamed.

Jesus pulls me into a comforting embrace. I sigh and lean into the hug, blocking out the roar rising again around me.

I gasp and tears stream down my cheeks. I grab the nearest pew, but it crumbles under my weight, throwing me off balance. I redirect my momentum forward, stumbling to the steps before the altar. There too, I crumble into a broken heap. The beams broken across the altar are a cross and Jesus is strewn across them. The base reaches down the steps while the top stretches over the altar. Nails are visible through Jesus' feet and wrists.

There at the foot of the cross, there at the feet of my Savior, I am a bumbling heap. Jesus is there on the cross, crucified before me and there is nothing I can do to help. His chest still slowly rises and falls, straining with the effort just to breathe, but I know the story, I know the end is coming soon.

As Jesus is lying there, something appears at the foot of the cross and curls up into a ball, yawning. It doesn't seem to notice the scene above it.

"Shoo, go away." I try to shoo it away with my foot. It looks at me indignantly with aqua eyes.

"What do you want?" I yell at it. "There are only seven deadly sins! What are you supposed to be? The ultimate sin?"

"Yes, in a way," Jesus says. My jaw drops at His response. And He should be saving His strength. I wasn't being serious. I… it wasn't like I killed anyone.

"That one"—He nods His head at the big unnamed one—"is the worst sin of the modern age." But He doesn't name it. The suspense is killing me as the silence draws on.

"What is it?" I timidly ask.

"Indifference, also known as 'that isn't my problem.'"

The demon opens its eyes and looks at me, yawns, and closes its eyes again. I kick it in anger. It jumps up and hisses at me, and then goes to find a different spot to curl up to sleep.

BRICE

I'm at a church event with a friend. There's a speaker on stage practically yelling at us. It would be disturbing except I agree with what he is saying. He's excited about chastity. It's encouraging someone else seems to get it. So many people are so fake when it comes to stuff like this; preaching and acting one way at church and another way somewhere else.

I look at Jesus, waiting for what I did or didn't do. I'm surprised when my friend breaks the silence. "Some people really need to hear this." He points a few rows in front of us and laughs at a girl sinking into her pew. "Someone probably did a walk of shame last night!" he laughs. To my dismay, the younger me joins in.

"That wasn't very nice," I say to Jesus. "I shouldn't have judged her... wait... I saw her... that morning? She was a mess."

I look at Jesus with my heart in my throat. "It wasn't a walk of shame, was it? Or I mean it wasn't—wasn't deserved. She... she's hurting so much. Why didn't I see it?" I'm stunned at my revelation.

"What's important is you do now," Jesus replies kindly.

As I look around the chapel, I can't believe the state it is deteriorating into. Chairs are flipped over now. This isn't a restful place. It's a mess.

"We'll fix it. Together. Be patient—"

"These things take time. I know," I sigh. I push some debris with the toe of my shoe. "I can't rest while I see this mess." Now I know there is something alive in the corner. It is unsettling. I did go to the right place after death? I wonder—

He smiles compassionately. "Not you, you don't rest while there's work to be done."

The church melts away into another scene. We're at—my heart sinks. We're at the office where I used to work, long ago. We're at my biggest failure.

My dad had broad theories about what success looks like, but few actual examples; my brother being his go-to. Everything Bryan did was perfect, even his mistakes. I did what I thought my dad wanted. I got a job. I worked hard. I did not get the promotions though. I guess I got so good at being invisible when I wanted to that I wasn't noticed when I needed it. I have always been an expert at being mediocre.

"Why here? What did I do wrong here?" I sigh.

"Nothing. You need to heal this hurt," Jesus replies.

"So—they were wrong." I could jump for joy.

He shakes his head and I'm instantly deflated.

"Then—who sinned?"

"It isn't always about sin, about who's right and who's wronged. It's about healing and you have a deep wound here."

I nod in agreement. I know exactly what He's talking about; I still feel it. "Where do I start?"

"Where the hurt is."

"So what do we need to talk about here?" I am still confused.

"What hurts?"

"I—um—nothing. It just didn't work out here. You said no one did anything wrong." My voice cracks at the last word.

He looks intensely at me.

"I—I failed. It proved I'm a disappointment. I was. Especially to my father. I"—I let out a long heavy sigh—"I never could make him proud of me. No matter what I did. But—but I know you'll tell me I'm wrong; he really was proud of me the whole time, it's all in my head."

"No."

"No? What? He wasn't—even deep down?" I try to choke back my tears. "He never really saw me, just what he wanted." I look down at my feet. Jesus nodded. "Parents can be blind like that sometimes. Your hurt is real. Your relationship with your father is still broken and we'll get to healing that—"

"So I have to let him back into my life? I thought—"

"You thought you'd end up in a better place than him."

"I—yeah."

"You don't have to let him back in to heal. You don't even have to see him. Not yet."

I let out a sigh of relief.

He laughs and continues, "This is about you. You need to heal."

I watch men and women shuffle back and forth with papers and folders in their arms. "This wasn't really where I wanted to be." I can see why they call it the rat race. An especially smug male coworker sits on the edge of a woman's desk. When she looks the other direction to grab something, he looks down her shirt. "This isn't *who* I wanted to be."

Jesus smiled softly. "You know who you are, my child. You always had that going for you."

I look over at the corner office. That oh-so-coveted space visible for all to admire but none but the elitist of the elite to achieve.

"I didn't just lose a dream. I lost who I thought I would become, who I thought I was. It wasn't just about a degree or a job, it was…"

"It is about who you are without titles and success."

"Yeah, I… I guess I don't really know who I am without all that."

"Bull."

"What?"

"You know who you are. It's… you don't know if you're worth anyone's time without the degrees and titles and jobs. If you have all that stuff, then you have to be worth everyone's time. Without it… you're not so sure."

"Yeah…"

"Now do you see it?"

"Envy. I was the one who sinned here. Always wanting… never getting fulfilled. I—I need to leave."

The bustle continues like buzzing insects swarming around me, threatening to swallow me up. I can't breathe. Do I need to breathe? I remember I'm already dead. I—

Jesus puts both hands on my shoulders. "Take a slow deep breath. Yes, you still breathe, in a way. It's not air like before—just breathe. Breathe in the Spirit."

I start to calm down.

"What was that?"

"I think it was a panic attack."

"I"—my heart sinks—"I can't escape anxiety even here?"

"You can't escape who you are."

183

"So I'm anxiety." I stare out the office building's window.

"No, but you need to accept that part of you. It's not some demon chasing after you. Feel how you feel and learn to let it go."

"I—"

"Feel better?"

"Yeah, it's passing, I think. I just can't believe I still have to deal with all that. I can't seem to escape it even in death."

"It's not about escaping. It's"—He takes my hands within His—"It's about being. Try to just be."

"I have no idea what that means."

"Embrace all the things We made you to be," Jesus explains.

"Envy, anxiety, failure. That's what I'm made of? No wonder I haven't moved on."

Jesus sighs and puts a hand on my arm, leading me in the other direction. We're back at the church. It is more of a mess than ever. Candles are knocked over, a windowpane is cracked, and a few chairs are tipped over. I can see the demons, though they keep their distance. Little gargoyles, the darkest black, but with beady eyes; a few even have wings. Defeated, I sit on a nearby chair that is mostly intact. Beams are strewn and scattered around. My tunic is torn to shreds across His body.

Jesus is standing in the front of the church talking to two men. A holy glow surrounds them. I do not know the other two before me. They have beards and look old and authoritative. Are they...?

184

Jesus seems to finally notice me. Correcting me, He says, "This is Moses"—one of the men nods—"and Elijah." The other nods.

I am awed by their presence. I have heard about these holy men, but now. How do I show reverence?

I duck my head feeling unworthy of eye contact. Do I kneel? Do I—but the light fades. I look up and see only Jesus is standing before me.

"I have to go," Jesus says.

"But—" I protest, but He puts a hand up silencing me.

I sulk by the steps, helpless. Something is wrong, I can feel it. How can I help? I can't. My head drops, but I also see something sleeping at the foot of the steps.

"Shoo!" I yell. It raises its head, glaring at me with turquoise eyes. "Shoo! You don't belong here! What are you even?"

"Indifference," Jesus says meekly.

"Indifference?" I echo.

"It is the gravest sin of this age," He murmurs.

"Indifference," I repeat again, then turn back to my Lord.

"I must go now," Jesus says and is gone.

I suppose other people need Him, too. I shouldn't be so selfish.

Chapter 16

"You shall cross the barren desert
But you shall not die of thirst
You shall wander far in safety
Though you do not know the way
You shall speak your words in foreign
lands
And all will understand
You shall see the face of God and live

Be not afraid
I go before you always
Come follow me
And I will give you rest"

Be Not Afraid by Bob Dufford, SJ

CATHERINE

There were a lot of little things that drove me away from the church. Though a picture came to mind of the final straw. I can remember it like yesterday, the smell and feel of the grass I am sitting on, a clear crispness on the breeze, the blinding brightness of the summer sun, the shade of the church building. I am a teenager trying to find my place, in my family, in the world, and in my church. The man is much older but doesn't seem all that wiser to be honest. He keeps a respectful distance and clearly does everything by the books. He definitely knows the rules, but not always in a good way. There are no grey areas in his life and I don't trust that; I don't believe that's possible in reality. We have some downtime before this year's summer bible camp that I'm volunteering at, and so is he.

I lounge around in the grass during a break with the others. A group of us are sitting there talking about nothing and everything. At first, I don't really chime into the conversation, but I am soaking it all in, chewing on my thoughts. I always like learning and gaining new perspectives, I like conversations though, not getting ideas rammed down my throat.

"...that's why the diaconate is important for married men to join."

I perk up; I read something recently about the early church having women deacons so maybe I have something to actually add.

"I don't see why women can't do it too, they used to do it in the early church. And it's not the same as being priests."

"That's a misinterpretation of the word deacon. It's not the same thing then as we understand it now. Women can't do that. And you should be happy singing in the choir."

'*This is where you turned away from God,*' I think to myself.

'*So I need to be forgiven for standing up for myself?*' I'm livid, but I try to calm down. I didn't mean to turn away from God, just from jerks like him. If my gaze could burn through him, he'd be nothing but ash at this point.

'*Catherine, you need to* heal *from this*,' I tell myself. I know it is what Jesus would say, so I— I have to tell myself it. I can get through this without Him. It's just for a little while.

I... I did. I moved on, got my mind back in the present, or past, or whatever is going on in front of me. I got over it. I came back to the church. Eventually.

Did you get over it though?

'*So I* still *need to put that jerk behind me? It's criminal that men like that can have so much power over me. Even here I can't get away from it*,' I steam.

I know it changed things, but it was one day. One conversation. He didn't really mean that much to my life, in the grand scheme of things.

'*Did it hurt*?' I ask myself. I have to look at it the way He would.

I—yes. It hurt. I deserve to be treated better than that. And not just by him, by my church. I can feel my anger rising again, so I take in a deep slow breath.

He pushed me away. Told me I didn't belong. That's not how you treat people.

I—lost a piece of myself. I felt out of place. All this about the 'body of Christ' and everyone has a place—where was my place? Where *is* my place?

I'm in another memory now. I'm in a new apartment and my neighbor stops by.

"Can we talk?" she asks me.

I have been slowly warming up to my neighbor Lisa, so I respond, "Sure."

"Why do you pray to them?" She nods to my saints' prayer cards on my desk and continues, "I mean Catholics aren't really Christians. You can't be since you worship Mary and the saints. And your communion—it's weird. And you don't let anybody else eat it. Besides, why would you believe in a church that puts down women and fought the crusades?"

"Well, first off, I don't pray *to* them. It's not like I worship them, it's… more like if I called you when I need prayers, to pray *for* me. It's… it's about connection." I pick up the St. Dymphna card and look at it as I begin again, "Connecting to something—someone important. Someone you know got it right, at least some of the time. So if they got it right, they'd know what to say and do, when I'm struggling and searching for God—searching for the right prayer; they'd be better at it than I am."

"I—oh," she says, "it's—that's not what I thought, but still, shouldn't you let the dead… rest?"

"It's—they—we all want connection. That doesn't end when we die," I say. "We're all connected this way." I smile and think about my grandmother. She may not have a prayer card, but I'm sure she had most things figured out.

"It says in Isaiah…"

But I shut down and don't even listen to her begin to lecture me on all the ways my faith is wrong. I've heard it before. I put the cards in the top drawer of my desk and think to myself that I never should have tried to explain it. Most people already have their mind made up what I should or shouldn't do, or pray to, or believe.

BRICE

The scene is changing again; it's a blur at first then recognition sets in. I'm on my mission. Even walking down the foreign streets, I didn't feel homesick; I was too caught up in how exciting every day was. This was another joyful time being of service to others, making a difference in the world, letting my faith be all-consuming in my life.

It's difficult work, trying to bring God's love to the world, but someone's got to do it. I work on being of service as well as spreading the good news. Actions speak louder than words after all. Every volunteer opportunity I hear about, I am the first to sign up. I help clean up files at a not-for-profit; I help pick up trash in a community clean-up day; I serve food at a town pancake breakfast. I mean I found the right way; I wouldn't want to rob anyone else of this joy out of ignorance. If they turn away, well then, that's their choice, but at least they had the chance. I know I'm called: be light, be salt, shout it from the mountain tops. God is so great, how could I not talk about it every chance I get?

I'm walking down a street halfway around the world. Soon I see a family walking toward us, but my heart sinks. Halfway around the world and I run into a family from down the street. I hope that a familiar face in a foreign land will help the conversation so I say, "Hello there, Mrs. McCarthy. Fancy meeting you out here."

"Hello, Brice. It's nice to see you too." Her voice is kind, but her smile is stern. "I'm sorry, we don't have time to catch up right now." She glances at my nametag. Then charges past with her husband and adult children in tow.

When she thinks she is out of earshot I hear her turn to her daughters and say, "We don't talk about our faith, *we* live it!"

She might as well have slapped me across the face, but it's only because she doesn't see what it is I really do on my mission. I'm sure if she would just open her eyes, have a conversation, look for the good at least. She'll change her mind, if not now, someday. I'll pray for her.

We go door to door the next day. The first house has a nice flowerbed near the porch. We knock and it opens.

"Yes?" a woman says, then her eyes appear to catch sight of our name tags as I am trying to introduce myself.

"I'm—"

But the door has already closed again.

We go to the next door but there is no answer.

The third house we go to has a TV on so loud I can hear it outside. We ring the doorbell, but there is no answer. We wait and try again, but only see the curtain shift a little.

The next house has a fenced yard we enter first, then approach the door. We ring the doorbell and a dog begins to bark. A big dog from the sound of its voice. I shift my weight a little nervously as the woman opens the door, clearly struggling to hold the dog back. It keeps hooking its nose around the door and pushing it open a little more.

"Have you heard of the Book of Mormon?" Elder Paul asks.

"Yeah, but I haven't read it," she says, then adds, "Just let me put the dog away."

I am comforted that it won't keep trying to get out the door, but I am also nervous as she struggles with its collar trying to pull it away. I wonder if getting mauled would count as martyrdom? Finally, the dog disappears into the house and the woman returns alone.

"I don't have a lot of time right now," she says when she returns, "but I'm willing to take a look if you have like a pamphlet or something."

"Could we set up a time to meet, when it is more convenient for you?" I ask, but I can see the hesitation in her face.

"I'll take a look…"

"Maybe we'll just leave you a number if you have questions," Elder Paul adds hopefully.

We both jot numbers down for her and turn to go to the next house.

Time and time again the door is slammed in our faces. People scurry about their busy lives, no time to talk about like things like religion or eternal salvation.

Scene after scene from that year flashes in front of me until I get to the one I wish I could skip over. It's not like I am visiting every second of my life. '*Why this? Why now? Why alone? Do I have any control over this*?' I wonder.

192

I'm in the apartment I'm sharing with the other missionary, but he is in his room and I'm alone in mine. It has been nine months of my mission, nine months of service, nine months of knocking on doors, nine months of deep prayer; yet what do I have to show for it? How many people have I actually saved?

Back at the chapel, things are really a mess.

"It was only a moment of weakness. Only one," I whimper, but there is a crash several yards in front of me. When the dust settles, I can see a hole in the ceiling and two beams have fallen through. Great, now the ceiling will crash down on me. This place is falling apart and it is all my fault. If only I had the faith of a mustard seed.

CATHERINE

I'm at the store, no, the pharmacy. This isn't where I thought I was going next, but okay. I mean, do I have a choice? I see myself coming up toward the counter then hesitating and turning back. I am trying to muster up the courage to actually go to the counter. My heart is in the very pits of my stomach. I know why I'm here.

"Really? This? You told me it wasn't my fault." I look up as if I can talk to Jesus through the ceiling.

"It was a health thing," I say defensively, though I am still standing there alone. I cross my arms and my head drops. "I… I didn't want to… I had to…"

The younger version of myself finally reaches the counter and hands over the prescription. The tech glances at the paper then stops and looks more intently, reading it. "We can't fill this," and he hands it back.

I am devastated. "I... but, my doctor..."

"You have other options you know," the pharmacy tech loftily replies.

"I... look this is between me and my doctor. He wrote me a prescription, so fill it!"

"It's murder," he replies and walks away from the counter. My face burns with anger. Luckily, someone else walks up to help me.

"So he was the one that was wrong!" I point at the counter. "Ha! Self-righteous jerk."

"Oh, I probably shouldn't react like that," I add sheepishly.

'*He did have good intentions*,' I tell myself, deflated.

"I... I was already ashamed. I didn't need all that. I... I had lost my baby, but"—I let out a long sigh—"my body... I had complications. It really wasn't his business. I don't have to prove it was a miscarriage. I needed that to... expel... I needed antibiotics too. Maybe if he wasn't so judgmental, he could have seen how much I was suffering."

Judgment hurts.

"Yeah, I was already hurting, but it was like getting sucker-punched on top of it. It made me so angry. It wasn't Brice's place to say that and walk away. What does he know about me or my life? I hated that guy; he was always annoying."

I'm back at the church, but still seething.

You 'always hated that guy'? Probably not my best response.

Well… I know hate doesn't belong in the kingdom of God. What was that verse…

Matthew 5:43-44: love your enemies and all that.

So, about all this hate. A rather large demon jumps out of a shadow startling me. It looks meaner than the other ones I've seen. I look at it and back at the altar. I look back and forth between the demon and around the room, and then again before it dawns on me.

"That's—that's my hate, that demon. Isn't it? Are you the one destroying this place?"

It growls in reply.

I take a deep breath. "Okay, I'm ready to face it." I have steel in my veins, so is my resolve. I can face anything.

His chest still rises and falls slowly and painfully. Maybe, just maybe, if I can reach Him and gently remove the pieces pinning Him to the cross… I rise and start to lean forward when—crash—a piece of the light fixture above Him suddenly breaks off and falls. With a sickening sound, it falls into His side. He cries out and is silent. The light around me flickers and goes out; the candles are left smoldering. Another crash, the altar cracks down the middle and falls in on itself. The last remnants of light through the windows also disappear as if clouds are gathering overhead. I am engulfed in darkness. I am alone, alone in my crumbling cathedral, my crumbling life. I fumble to the cross to sit and wait. I know what happens next. I just need to wait…

Alone in the darkness, I do the only thing I can think to do: I weep.

BRICE

I am not here to be condemned.

I brighten slightly, but still feel pretty miserable.

"What was the point of going on a mission?" I ask myself.

To bring Your love into the world, to open people's eyes to it. I look up at the broken ceiling above me.

And did I?

"I—I think so…" I tell myself hesitantly.

The short answer is yes… and no. And that is the point of all of this. He was working through me when I did bring His love—and when I didn't.

"Okay," I squeak. This is more difficult than I expected. Didn't I get it right sometimes too?

I'm in another memory now. I'm getting off the plane at home from my mission. I'm finally home! It's good to be home. And I'm so proud of the work I did. It's only… I know I don't have my family waiting for me like the others returning home. I look sadly around at the welcome home signs, not for me. I smile when I see the Johnsons. They have welcomed me since the first day I stepped foot inside the chapel. They welcome me like a son. I smile and tear up as I give Mrs. Johnson a hug. I do have a family after all. I'm walking through the airport with them when I see her. This stunning angel. I knew her in high school, but now that we're adults, I guess I really see her for the first time. I tell my pseudo-family I'll catch up in a minute.

I get up the courage and walk over to her. "Hi Sophie," I say with more confidence than I feel. She smiles at me and I know my world is complete. "Just getting home?" she says.

"Yeah," is all I can muster to say in response.

"I'd like to hear about it sometime," she says, leaving me swooning.

The chapel again is empty. When will He return? My heart yearns for His presence. I don't think I have ever felt so alone. There are baskets on the steps now. I peer into them and see fish in one, bread in the other. I walk away. I am not hungry and I want to get away from such mediocre Earthly needs. I should be beyond hunger now. Now, I am just so very, very alone. I curl up in a spot relatively free of debris and wait. If I wait, He is sure to come back. I just have to wait. In silence and near darkness. Alone.

Chapter 17

"All the promises I've broken
All the times I've let you down
You've forgot them but still I hold on
To the pain that makes me drown
Now, I'm ready
To let it go
To give it away

Take it all 'cause I can't take it any
longer
With all I have, I can't make it on my
own
Take the first, take the last
Take the good and take the rest
Here I am, all I have, take it all"

Take it All by Third Day

CATHERINE

I'm not where I should be. I thought death was next? The bar isn't where I 'caught' cancer. It was unhealthy for sure. Wait... my stomach sinks as the scene comes into focus. I know what night this is. I gulp.

Tony is just a little too loud, just a little too annoying, just a little too unsteady on his own feet, and way too drunk. I don't know what is coming—but I should have.

Tears spill out of my eyes. No! I know I shouldn't have let him leave! I wish I am really back in this night. If only I could change it…

"Come on Catherine," he whines again. "Just give me a ride home."

"I can't," I say. "I've been drinking too. And I'm just around the corner, I don't have to drive. Figure it out for yourself."

Why would I say that? I begin to cry. If I had only known what would happen that night, I never would have let him drive home. I would have called him a cab at least. I wouldn't have lied to him about being drunk.

I refuse to open my eyes again, sobbing; even after I know I'm back in the church, I won't open them. I can't face this.

Brice

'Why am I in a hospital?' I think, looking around. I died in the car, not here. Am I in the morgue or something? Did they at least try to save me? That's when I see her.

Catherine is in a hospital bed in a room nearby. I notice I'm standing near a nurse's station. *'I have no idea why I'm here,'* I keep repeating to myself.

"It's too bad she couldn't find a donor. She could have at least a few more years, maybe longer," one nurse says to another.

Is that it? I'm getting a guilt trip about not being an organ donor? Like my organs were any good after the accident anyway! So I can't even die the right way!

"Yeah, a bone marrow donor when a family isn't a match is one of the hardest donors to find."

I swallow hard, my anger is so misplaced. The guilt washes over me instead as I think of the health fair. I could have helped her. I should have helped her, years ago. My shoulders sink. I didn't even have to die to save her... to donate what she needed. She lived down the street from me. I had failed her so many times according to these memories and I failed her in the end too. I expect myself to cry, but the tears don't come. I am too miserable to even cry.

"I didn't know. How could I have known I could save her?" I cry out loud.

'*You knew you could have saved someone*,' I can't help but rebuke myself.

CATHERINE

I am alone again in the dark cathedral. I can feel the marble steps and feel my way through some drywall and wood and glass shards. I cut my hands on pieces of glass and metal, but I have to find it; I have to know I'm not alone. I know He isn't really dead, or I mean He was, but He rises. I try to think through it, but my head hurts and now my hands do, too.

I gasp as I stub my toe, but finally I find the wooden beam. Not caring about the splinters, I run my hand up the beam. If I can just touch His foot, His calf, His hand that has held mine so tenderly; but my hand only finds wood. My fingers fumble across the board sideways, maybe I'm over farther than I think. Still, nothing but broken wood. I feel up the beam, maybe I'm lower than I think. I feel a glimmer of reassurance until I find the crossbeam and still, it is empty. I reach across. If the altar isn't there, then maybe it's the wrong pieces of wood, but sure enough, I find the cold stone just where I expect to. I sit beside the cross, defeated when I feel a familiar warmth by my leg. Then another. Of course, my demons come to visit at a time like this.

BRICE

The chapel is empty and broken. I don't know whether to laugh or cry at this mess; this mess that is my life. Was my life, crumbling around me. There is something laying on the top step. I walk up to it and it looks like a body under a white cloth. I hesitate, but I must do… something. With a trembling hand, I pull the cloth back to reveal the face. It is someone I don't recognize. No, wait. It changes, transforms before my eyes. I am looking at my own dead face. So this isn't my body I am walking around in; it only feels like I'm touching things! I turn away. A wind seems to pass by me with a whoosh. I hear the cloth rustle, so I turn to grab it, to be respectful and cover the body, but it's gone. The body, my body, is gone and a white sheet is blowing and dancing in this new wind.

There are letters carved into the floor where the carpet has pulled away. Lazarus, they say.

Suddenly darkness falls around me. I try to find the steps in front of me, to sit.

I yell out, trying not to curse as my toe throbs. I found the steps.

I reach down to see what my toe collided with; it is a wooden beam from the ceiling, leaning upwards. I bet it's the one that formed the cross, I think. I reach next to it and find the steps. I am comforted by some orientation, though I still can't see a thing around me. I keep seeking, moving slowly in the dark. My heart jumps to my throat as I find another piece of wood in front of me. The crossbeam is in my left hand and it is also empty. I sit and put my head in my hands. I can't help it; right now in the dark, it seems so hopeless. Something warm and scaly rubs against my leg. I don't try to shoo it away this time. What's the point anyways?

Chapter 18

"Why, why are you still with me?
Didn't you see what I've done?
In my shame I want to run and hide
myself
But it's here I see the truth
I don't deserve you

But I need you to love me, and I
I won't keep my heart from you this
time
So I'll stop this pretending that I can
Somehow deserve what I already have
I need you to love me

I, I have wasted so much time
Pushing you away from me
I just never saw how much you could
cherish me
Cuz you're a God who has all things
And still you want me."

I Need You to Love Me by BarlowGirl

CATHERINE

"I killed him," I say miserably. "I mean I didn't, but I did… I will need to face him."

I think about the other scenes from my life. "He was important—is important to my life, isn't he?" I realize.

Suddenly, I'm at the hospital. At my end. I only know it's the day I die by guessing, but what else could it be? Everything in my hospital room looks like it did day in and day out; family comes in shifts so I'm not alone. I stand looking at myself and just want it to be over. After all, to me, I'm already dead. Seconds tick away; minutes stretch on into hours in the deathwatch. The people around me are the only noticeable changes.

"I'm… I'm not sure why I'm here," I whimper.

Finally, it is Gracie's turn to sit by my side, signaling the end is near.

It is late. Gracie is sitting in the chair nodding off, clearly exhausted as her head droops again and again.

A nurse enters and pulls Gracie aside.

"Go get a coffee. I'll stay with your mom so she isn't alone," she says kindly.

"No, I couldn't," Gracie protests, but the nurse insists. Gracie stands. "I'll be *right* back," she says.

I am left with the nurse and the ever beeping, sighing, and flashing machines. They keep me tethered to every last morsel of life. The nurse tenderly brushes what is left of my hair out of my face and sits in the chair by the bedside.

"It's too bad we found the donor too late," she says more to herself than to me.

My eyes widen. "What did she say?" I turn, then remember I am alone. "They found a donor? But too late! Too late in my disease…"

"It's too bad he died a few years ago. He died while you were in remission."

"How did you know?" I don't know why I ask; she can't hear me.

"He was an organ donor and was entered into the registry. It was a mistake that he remained in the database after he died," she explains, "but that's just between us."

"So it wouldn't have mattered," I grumble. "There's no use dwelling on it though."

"It would have mattered if he joined the registry years ago, before your remission, then you could have been cured through a bone marrow transplant."

"Would have… could have…. What would it matter? He didn't make me sick. So he didn't save a stranger? So what?" I say while I feel completely miserable. "I'm still not sure why I'm here."

I don't know how I'm having a conversation with someone who can't see or hear me.

I sit in the far chair in silence and watch. Any time now, Gracie will come back and I will die.

The change in the beeping signaling the end rings out, but where is she? I know I heard Gracie before the end. Maybe I just imagined it. The nurse rushes to check my vitals to confirm the alarms as a doctor rushes in. They bustle around me as Gracie enters the room again.

Tears well in her eyes as she raises her hands to cover her mouth.

"Mom!" she cries out, then she whispers, "She's gone… she's really gone," and she staggers out of the room. She walks out into the hallway to call her father. I can gather enough from her side of the conversation that he is agreeing to tell other family members. '*Poor Tim,*' I think. There is so much on his shoulders right now. Then, to my surprise, Gracie makes another call.

"She's gone. My mom died," she squeaks out through her tears.

"No," she continues, "I didn't get a chance to tell her we're getting married." She breaks into sobs and that's when I see the ring on her left hand.

I sit in a chair just inside the hospital room as staff continue to bustle around me.

"I won't be there. I'm dead, so I won't be at my daughter's wedding," I say solemnly. I am quietly waiting for a comforting word that doesn't come.

After some silence, I continue, "But I could have been. I could have been there if this guy had signed up on a stupid registry years ago!" I raise my hands to my face, then run them through my hair. "Who was he anyway? Better not have been someone I knew," I storm.

I walk up behind the nurse and peek over her shoulder. Sure enough, she is holding the registry as well as my file. I see a name clearly printed with a single line through it, probably indicating he is no longer available.

'Brice,' it reads.

My hands fall to my side. This can't be happening.

BRICE

"I could have saved her," I say, finally letting go of my excuses. "I failed her." My shoulders hunch forward, my head is in my hands. I raise my head, so my hands are hiding my mouth. Through my fingers, I mumble, "I need to see her, don't I? To—to make it right?"

Suddenly, I'm at a bar.

"What are we doing here? I never set foot in here!" I protest.

A man is just entering the bar but is already stumbling, drunk.

I can't believe my eyes. I don't know the man. I wish I knew his name, but that face. The face I saw get out of his car and look right at me, before getting back into his car and driving away. The man who left me to die. Is this the night he kills me?

I am overcome with anger. Why? How could he? I take a deep breath. I look up to the heavens, furious.

"Why am I here?" I manage to say through gritted teeth. "Because I need to forgive to move forward? I can't forgive him." I'm shaking a little. "Not yet," I whimper.

My eyes are drawn to where the man goes to sit at a table with a woman. There is a lump in my throat. She is a woman I know.

"Not now, Tony," she says to him.

"Come on, Catherine," he whines again. "Just give me a ride home."

"What does Catherine have to do with anything?" I say coolly, but the scene is already playing out in front of me.

"I can't," she says. "I've been drinking too. And I'm just around the corner, I don't have to drive. Figure it out for yourself."

I stand there, stunned.

"So she—she could have stopped him?" I say hoarsely. "I didn't have to die." I slide into a chair and put my head in my hands. "She could have saved me and I—I could have saved her. I guess it's what we both deserve then."

"Can't we just skip to Your resurrection?" I blurt out.

I am troubled by the thought of being alone through this, but I'm never alone.

'*For now, focus on Catherine*,' I think. One step at a time.

I take a deep breath and look up at Catherine laughing and joking with some other friends, oblivious to Tony as he stumbles to the door. He stops at a table by the door for a moment to regain his balance. I look back at Catherine.

Okay, what do I need to do? Only I can really answer that. I have a lot to forgive, in her and in myself. I'll have to think about what that will take.

CATHERINE

Death is inevitable; it happens to everyone sometime. The whole time I am sick, I comfort myself by saying we did everything we could:

me, the doctors, nurses, my family, everyone I knew. Except one. There was someone, somewhere who didn't do enough. All they had to do was sign up as a donor, give a little blood sample.

While I was sick, the only words that give me comfort were from the Dalai Lama. He wrote, "Illness happens. It is not something exceptional; it is part of nature and a fact of life. Of course, we have every right to avoid illness and pain, but in spite of that effort, when illness happens it is better to accept it. While you should make every effort to cure it as soon as possible, you should have no extra mental burden... 'If there is a way to overcome the suffering, then there is no need to worry; if there is no way to overcome the suffering, then there is no use in worrying.'"[2]

I thought there was no use in worrying, but it turns out I was wrong. It all could have been different.

BRICE

I'm back at the chapel, but refuse to look around. I know what a mess I've turned my life into. I sit in stunned silence. I knew I didn't have to die; any accidents could be prevented. I knew that if only things had been a little different, I would still be alive. I didn't know how close she came to saving me. If only, if only she knew. I have a family I was torn away from!

Chapter 19

"Oh, to grace how great a debtor
Daily I'm constrained to be
Let that goodness like a fetter
Bind my wandering heart to Thee
Prone to wander, Lord, I feel it
Prone to leave the God I love
Here's my heart, oh, take and seal it
Seal it for Thy courts above"

Come Thou Fount

CATHERINE

I'm alone in my memory now. It's the bathroom in my old apartment. Carefully, I approach the shower and peek around the curtain. I see my face turned downward. Tears mix with water as they stream down my cheeks. I reach up and put a hand on my cheek. My face changes. I sigh deeply and stop crying. '*Maybe this is why I'm here,*' I think. '*I am here to help myself.*'
I'm not sure what day it is or what's going on at all. I have no guide with me this time. I am alone with myself.
I walk out of the bathroom as the younger me turns the water in the shower off. I walk over to

my dresser. I look at my trinkets, my hairbrush. I touch my necklace from my mother, my ring from my father. I look at the empty mirror sadly. I'm not really here, am I? I look at the pictures along the side of the mirror. A postcard from our trip overseas, a picture of my parents and myself at graduation, finally a picture of me and Jenn. I touch the image of her face.

"I just want to be with you," I whisper.

"Hey there, sexy." I suddenly hear a voice that makes bile rise in my throat.

BRICE

I'm driving now. It's just me and myself.

I sit in the backseat and watch my younger self like I'm a taxi driver. It's not the day I die, I can tell from my shirt. From what I can tell, it's just an ordinary day. We cross the bridge over the interstate. I look out the window at the spot I once thought about jumping off into traffic below.

From the front seat, I let out a sigh, but I just keep driving. I always have to keep going.

It turns out I'm driving to work at the pharmacy. Like a ghost, which I guess you could say I am, I pass through the car door to follow myself. I go into the back, ready to start my day, but the present me doesn't follow. I am distracted by one of the aisles I pass. I'm by the liquor aisle and a now-familiar face has caught my eye. Tony, as she called him, is standing by the liquor bottles, debating his purchase.

"I shouldn't," he mumbles.

Damn straight you shouldn't!

He walks away a few steps, only to turn around and return to the same spot.

"Just one—no! Not even one." He walks away.

I start to—to feel sorry for him as he paces, twitching. He shakes his hands and finally walks away. I feel relieved, proud even. '*Why do I feel anything but angry*?' I think suddenly. I know he's going to drink again! My temper grows into a crescendo and I turn and punch a wine bottle. To my great surprise I sort of connect with it; not like if I had punched it when I was alive, but it does shift and slips off the shelf. A woman passing by shrieks and jumps back, looking bewildered.

CATHERINE

I am so angry when I hear Theodore's voice. He doesn't belong here! He—he—I can't even think straight I'm so angry. I pull my hand back from the picture of Jennifer and my nostrils flare. I slam my hand down on the dresser but jump back as the dresser shakes from the impact. I hit it. I really hit it. Theodore walks into the room.

"Come on babe," he whines.

Maybe…

I pull my arm back and put my all into swinging at him, but my fist passes right through him and I am thrown off balance and tumble to the floor. I grumble. What am I supposed to do now?

'*Wait, maybe I can get rid of him*!' I say to myself, thinking of how to haunt him.

"Catherine, come here baby," he whines.

"Get out!" the younger me yells.

From the floor, I smile. I don't need to do a thing. "Seriously," the younger me reiterates. "I met someone. Someone I really like. I think I have a chance to be happy with Tim. So *get out*!"

"But we could have one last fling?" he weasels. Even wrapped in the towel, I go to my front door and open it.

"Go. Now!"

"Okay, okay," he says and walks to the door finally. "Just one last—"

I slam the door in his face. I lock it this time. I slide down the door into a heap on the floor crying.

My ghost self goes over to the heap and I try to put my hand on my younger self's cheek again, but it doesn't work this time. I'm on my side and I curl up into the fetal position still crying.

"But you're free," I tell the crying heap, "you're finally free. Tim is good for you. You'll be happy."

Angry, my ghost self stands up, glaring at the door. I take a deep breath, then run through it. Much to my surprise, I pass easily through it. I thought I would at least feel it like when I touch something. When I regain my composure, I look around. I spot Theodore getting into his truck. I head over to it, not sure what I am going to do when I get there. What can I do?

I stand next to the driver's window, invisible. He is just sitting in the truck. It would be quite creepy, if he could see me that is, how close I am to him. He has his head in one hand and is looking down.

"Now what do I do?" I hear him mutter to himself.

"Pathetic," I spit out at him, but my shoulders drop, deflated. "What a sad, sad, little man you are after all," I say.

He puts the truck in reverse and drives away, leaving me standing there alone.

"You know," I say to myself, "I think I feel sorry for him."

I am again in the dark church, though a hole has opened above me. I can see stars shining down through the opening. The little light is comforting in this deep, deep darkness. I sit back so I can see them more clearly. I can count about twenty distinct stars and possibly some fainter ones. I don't recognize the constellations, though I only know a few, so it would be easy for me to miss a common one. The stars truly look close enough for me to reach up and touch.

A sudden splash startles me from my reverie. I sit up and am surprised I can see the water of the baptismal font a few yards away, down the center aisle. The light of the stars is reflected on the water's surface, making it visible in the darkness. The water is rippling and reflecting the starlight and twinkling as it hits the marble sides of the font. I rise and slowly walk through the debris, careful not to trip or stumble. I reach the edge and cautiously look over the water. The body of Jesus is laying at the bottom of the font! Even though the basin is small, I can see Him when I look into the water. I step back and look down at the wooden base of the font, then back into the basin. This is like some weird

214

magic or science fiction movie. There isn't room for a body in there! And yet, there He is. As I stand there staring, I feel a tug at my sleeve. I draw back and look at the glowing eyes around me.

"Not now," I shoo them back. I need to get Him out of the water. He doesn't belong in there. It isn't right. I'm not sure what will happen to a body left in water, but I think it's gross if I remember my cop and crime shows. He needs to be attended to, in the tomb, and then on the third day, He rises. I reach over the edge quickly before the little claws can reach out again, though I hear them screeching behind me. I don't turn at the noise but touch the water instead. As soon as I touch it, I feel something inside me change. A warmth surges through me, but I am also unable to pull my arm back. My eyes widen as I am drawn into the water. My whole arm is submerged, yet I do not touch the ceramic bottom nor the body I saw in the water. I gasp in a breath as my head is pulled under. I am completely under the water, flailing and turning. I turn toward the bottom, but the body is gone and only blackness is below me. I can't see the bottom. I cannot be in the baptismal font, clearly; the water goes much deeper. I turn toward the surface again and see pink, red, orange, yellow, green, blue, purple and teal eyes around a rectangle hole above me. What happened to the small circle I just passed through? I reach up to pull myself out again only to touch a solid surface, like ice, but not as cold. And the water is still making waves. How can a solid surface move like that? I pound and bang on the surface, to no avail. My breath escapes in bubbles and I start to see black spots. Maybe it's the spots in my vision, but I think I see someone standing on the surface above me as the spots grow together.

BRICE

I'm still standing in the liquor aisle of the drug store stunned. I wish I could help Susan, the store clerk tasked to clean it up.

"I'm sorry," I say to her as she sweeps up the broken glass. With an apologetic half-smile, I turn around and leave the aisle from the other side. I'm not sure why, since I typically walk through things, but I don't want to make her clean up job any harder than it already is. I spot Tony again, so I walk up to him.

"Do you even know what you've done—er, what you're going to do?" My anger loses steam as I realize he has no idea because it hasn't happened yet. I'm working over at the pharmacy.

"Well, you will. You'll be sorry! You'd better be sorry!" I yell at him. "What's the use?" I say to myself. I look down and sulk. That's when I notice his limp and I start to feel some empathy.

"Me too," I say. I wonder how he got his limp.

"You okay?" the cashier asks him, also noticing the limp.

"Yeah, I had a work accident. 'Bout a year ago. Still flares up sometimes," Tony says, avoiding eye contact with the cashier. He adds, "It hurts sometimes but… it means I can predict the weather." He tries to laugh it off.

Pain. I finally get it. He's trying to numb the pain. My shoulders drop as I—I feel sorry for what Tony must be going through.

I am in darkness again, though I can see some stars twinkling above me. A hole seems to have opened in the ceiling above me all the way through the roof. Even though it is clearly more concerning damage to the building, it is comforting to see the stars again. A twinkle in front of me draws my attention down again. The baptismal font is nearly ten feet away and reflecting the starlight. Drawn to it, I rise and pick my way through the debris. As I reach the basin, I see green, red and yellow eyes around me. The others appear one at a time until there are eight different colors of glowing eyes around me.

"Don't even think about it," I snap, and they scurry back a few steps. I lean over the font and peer into the water. The water doesn't stop at the font's bottom. I pull back and look at the sides of the font again. It is somewhat unnerving to see something inside that could not possibly fit the dimensions of the outside. I peer in the basin again and I do see a bottom and that's when I see Him! Somehow there is a body at the bottom: *His* body. I reach over the water but pull back when I hear a terrible scream. I scowl and reach out again. I will not be deterred by demons! I am filled with a deep warm, calming feeling as I touch the water. A gentle ripple starts at my touch, hits the side of the basin, and bounces back, but bigger. It rebounds again and again. Soon the water is roaring and splashing. I try to pull my hand back, but I can't. Instead, to my dismay, I am being pulled into the water. Fearful I will lose my arm, but unsure what to do, I look around frantically. This can't be right! With a gasp and a splash, I am pulled under the water. Due to my moment of panic, I fail to take a breath before my head is submerged, leaving me little time. I look down and see only an inky depth of water below. The body is gone. I turn above again, but there is glass or some other smooth surface blocking my retreat. How is this possible? It's moving in waves, but it's solid as a rock! I claw at it, but there isn't a crack or flaw to get my nails into. I gasp and choke on the water as feet appear above me, clearly walking on the water's surface. Hope springs inside me again. Only one person can walk on water. I know who is standing above me.

Chapter 20

"I know what you are like!
But I will heal you, lead you,
*   and give you comfort,*
until those who are mourning
*   start singing my praises.*
No matter where you are,
I, the Lord, will heal you
*   and give you peace."*

Isaiah, 57:18-19

CATHERINE

I'm still struggling and pounding on the barrier at the surface of the water as my field of vision narrows. The water is swirling and crashing around me. Even though the surface is impenetrable, it is a chaotic mess of waves and riptides. The only calm is a small circle around the feet-shaped shadows above me. '*This is it*,' I think. Wait, I'm already dead, I remember.

A hand reaches down and is suddenly through the barrier. It sits motionless and open in front of me. I just look at it, puzzled, as my hands still connect with something solid above me. I'm not sure how to get out of this on my own, so I guess I have to trust whoever this is…

I reach and fumble for a moment in the swirling water, then finally our hands connect. I am pulled through water—only water, no barrier—to the surface.

I am pulled up and sit on the side of a basin as I choke and sputter. I desperately try to dry my face, but as every inch of me is drenched and there is nothing within reach to help me, I am left with my own sopping wet hands to try to clear my vision. Finally, enough water drips away for my eyes to focus on something other than droplets. I realize I am in an unfamiliar font. It is clearly a baptismal font, but it is much larger than the one I entered. Where am I? As I ponder the impossibility of my experience, I fall backward, and I hit my arm and my back hard on broken wood and sheetrock in a pile behind me.

"Wait, where am I? That wasn't"—I don't want to finish my thought out loud and now I'm scared to look around. If that wasn't my font, what if this isn't my church? Can I visit someone else's purgatory? Whose? I hear another splash across the room.

BRICE

The water churns and crashes around me, knocking into me and pulling me. '*No*,' I think, '*I can't move*.' I frantically tread water. '*I can't lose sight of Him above me*'. If I just have enough faith…

220

I see His shadow bend down and break the barrier though the smooth water surrounding His feet. His hand is before me if I can just grab ahold. The water tosses me to and fro, making the still hand nearly impossible to get ahold of. Finally, I am able to connect and He pulls me out of the dark, stormy water. I feel a ledge behind me so I sit with my feet still in the water. Suddenly I remember my first experience touching the water here and quickly swing my legs out and to the other side.

Wait, this isn't right! Water droplets are making it hard to focus my eyes and I'm still coughing up water, gasping for breath. Finally, my vision comes into focus again and I see marble below me. Why am I sitting on marble? And it's small, like impossibly small, how are my legs still in the water when it's a tiny basin? Where… where am I? I start to panic.

CATHERINE

I take a deep breath and open my eyes. I have to face my surroundings at some point. Some things around me are starting to look familiar, but they are mixed and mashed up with unfamiliar details too. The broken pews are intermingled with darker ones, and broken chairs, like someone patched this place together with different woods and cut random holes in the pews to make room for the chairs. There are carpet patches as well as the marble floor. The walls, the ceiling, the windows all are a combination of old and new; familiar and alien, although all are tattered and broken. I can see the Eucharistic table Jesus and I shared is this same mismatch combination of our table and an unfamiliar one. There are still statues of the saints and the remnants of the Stations of the Cross on or near the far wall, but there is also a table with the legs missing on one side so it's partially on the ground. And what's that white statue? I can't tell from here, but I think maybe it's Jesus. I turn again and the altar that was broken during the crucifixion now is standing again. It appears to be patched with a wooden altar, combining it with the marble one.

Finally, I spot the baptismal font in the other main aisle, and that's when I see I'm not alone in this hodge-podge church.

BRICE

I try to lean back, my shoulders heaving, all of my body shivering. I place my head in my hands while I catch my breath. I just need a little time. I can figure out how to get back; I know I can. I just need to think clearly. Instead, I topple over like a cartoon character who realized they are balancing impossibly over a cliff. With a crash and a splash of water, I hit the ground hard and see spots in my vision.

Slowly, my vision comes back into focus more and more with each breath. That's when I notice a carpet patch a few feet away. It's not thrown on top of the marble floor, but set in among it. I crawl over to it, interested. The floor is level whether it's marble or carpet, like the dividing line between two rooms. Up close, the carpet is very familiar. It is a pattern I know very well. I reach and it feels familiar too. It is *my* carpet. It is from *my* chapel. I roll on my back and I see *my* ceiling… alongside unfamiliar broken rafters. I look above my head and the sacrament table is all wrong—well, partially wrong, making it all wrong. *My* table isn't past the steps and it isn't caved in on itself anymore. It is standing proud but with unfamiliar stone pieces. I turn to one side and I spot a broken chair among the pew across from me. It's *my* chair, well, one from my chapel. And the pews are some are *my* pews or pieces of them. Now that I see it, I spot other broken chairs and pieces of pews I recognize. I see more and more of my details around me along with the unfamiliar ones. I sit up, curious at the change in my surroundings. I see another main aisle at a 45-degree angle toward the front of the chapel, like the aisle I'm sitting in. In that aisle I see *my* baptismal font but—I'm not alone.

Chapter 21

"The Lord is extending the Saints'
understanding,
Restoring their judges and all as at
first.
The knowledge and power of God are
expanding;
The veil o'er the earth is beginning to
burst."

The Spirit of God

CATHERINE

I'm shouting at him now. "What have you done?"
I yell. Instead, I turn around to let my anger stew
among the statues I recognize. Eight shadows
jump out and run at the mess instead. I turn and
see eight unfamiliar, but similar and just as fast
creatures jump out of the shadows between him
and my demons. Sixteen moving shadows
stand facing off, growling and scratching at the
ground ready to fight.
A man I hadn't noticed and don't recognize rises
to his feet from the steps leading to the altar.
Even though I don't recognize him, he seems
familiar somehow. He walks between the two

battlefronts of the demons. Each creature he passes instantly calms at his presence. Of my line of defense, one lays down for a nap, two groom themselves, and one sits and turns around, looking intently at me. The others are slower to let up the fight but begin to reduce their signs of hostility. The other battlefront is a mirror image of the ones in front of me.

I look at the man intently. "Who are you?" I ask nervously.

He smiles. "Do you not recognize me?" He replies, "I am the one who has risen from the dead."

BRICE

Even though His appearance has changed, of course, it is Jesus standing between us. He's sure to understand this mess around us and fix it.

"She doesn't belong here," I spit out, then remember Jesus saying I would meet her at some point. Deflated somewhat, I continue, "There's some mistake with—with—look around!"

"Hmph," she says, but I ignore her and turn to Him.

"There's no mistake," He says.

"So I'm what? Supposed to help her? I'm sure there's something I can do."

"Excuse me!" she exclaims.

"I'm not talking to *you* at the moment," I snap, thinking about her friend driving drunk.

"Well if you need me"—she walks over to a row of battered statues—"I'll just be over here by St. Jude, the patron of lost causes and hopeless cases!" She plops down in the far aisle out of sight. Her posse of demons follows her and makes a protective semicircle around her.

I turn back to the transformed Jesus.

"What?" I ask when I see the way He's looking at me.

"You're both here to heal," He says kindly, "and forgive."

I think about Tony, but also about the bone marrow donation registry.

"Does she know?" I look at Jesus sadly.

"Yes," He replies, "but there's more to both of your stories than the endings."

It dawns on me. "She *was* in just about everything we've talked about so far."

Jesus nods.

"We—we both do have a lot to forgive," I say, looking down.

Jesus smiles. "And to be grateful for."

I think about the interstate overpass and about my daughter.

"What do I need to do?" I ask.

"It's not just about you anymore. It's about what you *both* need now."

CATHERINE

I listen to the conversation Brice is having with Jesus. It's hard not to. Typical, thinking he has a monopoly on what's right. At least Jesus isn't taking his side.

Brice comes over to me. "Look I think we got off on the wrong foot," he says.

"You think?" I snap back. "You tripped over the baptismal font!"

"Look that was an accident. It wasn't—urgh, why are you so—so…"

"So difficult?" I finish for him.

He softens his expression when he sees my face downcast.

"Don't worry, it isn't you," I say. "I can't help it I guess." I look up, but away from him. I can't bear to look at him.

"It's okay," Brice says kindly. When I roll my eyes, he continues, "No, really." He sits down beside me. "It's okay… to stop putting up a front. Just be you."

"Easy for you to say," I sigh. "You just don't get it."

"Then explain it to me," Brice snaps back, "it's not like I'm going anywhere!"

I roll my eyes again, but then take a deep breath. "I'm too much."

"You're…?" Brice questions, "Maybe you're around the wrong people?" he suggests. "The right people wouldn't tell you 'you're too much.'"

"It didn't matter who. It didn't matter when. They don't stick around. Tim did, but even he had limits to how much of me he could tolerate." When Brice looks confused, I add, "My husband, but that's not the point. People get a real glimpse of me and they run not walk. I'm—I was always too much."

"It can't be that bad," Brice says.

"I feel too deeply so I'm overdramatic; I'm too sad so I'm pessimistic; I'm angry when I'm hurt so I'm too sensitive; I'm lonely so I'm too clingy; I worry so I'm too anxious; I'm too hyper so I'm exhausting; I have too much on my mind so I'm scatterbrained; I have my mind made up so I'm too opinionated; I'm determined to succeed so I'm too career-driven; I'm still grieving so I'm stuck in the past; I'm creative so I'm too eccentric; I'm passionate so I'm too intense. And that's all in one day, so yeah. I *am* too much!" I throw my arms up. "I'm too much to be cooped up into one person!"

Brice doesn't say anything, but he scoots closer to me, practically on top of me!

"What are you doing?" I ask him.

"You said people run away when you're too much and… and I'm trying to show you I'm not going anywhere."

"That's… that's actually very sweet," I say and lay my head on his shoulder.

"Oh, that's not—"

"It's not like that for me either," I interrupt. I am distracted by a demon coming up to me though, so I move onto my hands and knees and approach it.

I reach my hand out to my demon with the pink eyes. It purrs and nuzzles up to my hand. I think about what Jesus said about it being a part of me, *the* part of me that wants to be loved. I plop down onto my stomach still playing with the demon. He's right; there is a part of me that would do *any*thing to be loved; to not be too much for once. This little goblin has gotten me into tough situations and it's difficult to accept this part of me, but…

I get it. Love feels good. It's also hard to believe I'm worthy of being loved. I have to earn it somehow. The demon looks deep into my eyes with its rosy ones. It squeaks and I think it smiles. It is hard to tell with such a grotesque mouth. It walks toward me until our eyes are so close they almost touch. It points its front leg at my heart.

"You want to go back?" I'm not sure why I asked that, but I think we understand each other now. It nods and takes a step toward me. All I see is a bright pink light and then nothingness.

BRICE

I'm caught up in my own thoughts about what is supposed to happen next when a bright pink light catches my eye. I look up and see a demon attacking Catherine.

"No," I yell and step toward her, but the light is so bright I have to look away. When I can look at her again, she's lying on the ground and the pink-eyed demon isn't anywhere in sight.

I rush over to her side.

"I'm okay," she says, as I reach down to prop her up. "Really, I—I feel better actually."

She is sitting now. "We need to be made whole again," she says.

"What?" I ask.

"The demons are a part of us. We accept them back into ourselves and we will be made whole again."

I sit back. "I can't"—but I change my mind—"What do I need to do?"

"Pick one," she says, "start off easy. Which one do you understand?"

I look at the creatures that followed me to her side. I spot the one with green eyes.

"Come here," I say to it.

Cautiously, it approaches me.

"I'm sorry," I say to it. "I've kicked it," I say with an apologetic half-smile to Catherine.

"Ah," she says, "I think I was the opposite, trying to be too nice and tame them or something."

I ponder her approach. "Did it help?"

"Not really," she says, "but at least mine aren't scared of me."

Finally, my envy is right in front of me. It sits, cocks its head to one side and looks intently at me.

"Now what?" I ask her.

"Get eye to eye with it and—I don't know how to explain it," she sighs, "accept it."

I look at the ground but decide to hold my hands out instead. It cautiously steps forward and I pick it up, raising it to eye-level. Its emerald eyes gaze deeply into mine.

"Ready?" I ask it.

It smiles an eerie, but slightly comical grin and nods yes. I take a deep breath, close my eyes, and say, "I accept you."

Nothing happens.

I open my eyes disappointed. Why is this so hard?

Chapter 22

"And love will hold us together
Make us a shelter weather the storm
And I'll be my brothers' keeper
So the whole world will know that
we're not alone"

Hold Us Together by Matt Maher

CATHERINE

"So why envy?" I ask Brice, trying to be helpful.
"My brother was always the one everyone loved.
I never seemed to live up to his shining example.
Especially at the office I worked at for a while,"
Brice explains.
"I remember. Wait, so you don't have anything
you're proud of? Like not a single thing you've
done?"
"Well, no," he admits. "I worked hard, but... it
just never really came together for me. Not like
it was supposed to."
"And you kept at it? You realize that's the
definition of insanity."
"Yeah I guess," he chuckles. "I just kept thinking
something's got to come together and it didn't
so I... I just had to figure something else out.
What, was I going to give up? I have a family to

think about, not just myself. Or had. Anyway, some people get the breaks, some don't." His voice breaks at these last words. He looks away from me, trying to be stronger than this.

"It's okay to be sad," I say. "Your life didn't go the way you wanted."

He hesitates, then looks me in the eye. Tears are in my eyes and he can see I understand. Finally, someone understands how difficult it is to keep trying to be strong. I'm not psychic, but I'm sure that's what we both are thinking. You can only be strong for so long. With all I have been through, of course I understand that.

"I just wanted to make something of myself; to show everyone they were wrong; show them I was a someone. I"—he sucks in a deep breath—"I wanted someone to be proud of me. To be... to be worth loving. A success, a someone, that is the guy everyone wants to be. To..."

"To make everyone else jealous."

"Yeah." He looks down, ashamed.

"But that isn't love." Even I know that.

"What?"

"You glossed over it, but you said you wanted to be worth loving."

"Yeah"—he suddenly looks defensive—"so what?"

"Jealousy isn't love. Love is patient, love is kind. It isn't jealous—"

"I know the verse," he snaps.

"I wonder..." I pause and let out a little sigh. I am a little afraid of getting snapped at again. He softens his expression when he realizes this. I continue, "I wonder who told you that you weren't loveable."

"What? No one would say a thing like that!"

"Not outright, people say a lot more than just... you know, the *words* that come out. Sometimes—no, pretty much all of the time there's things underneath. Sometimes we mean it and sometimes we don't. Sometimes we accidentally send the wrong messages under it all. Sometimes, though, people are just jerks."

BRICE

I look at the demon again and think about my brother. I think about the job I didn't get. I think about the love I didn't get. I think about the popularity I didn't have when I was younger. I look my envy in the eyes and I understand. I understand that I want what I can't have, what wasn't made for me. I understand I have a hole inside myself because of that longing, but what I want is not what will fill that hole.

A green light slowly grows from the demon's eyes and soon it surrounds and engulfs me. Then I see and experience nothing.

CATHERINE

The light is blinding again, but green this time. Then it is gone as suddenly as it appears. It takes several more minutes before my vision is normal. I didn't close my eyes, since he seemed to be having difficulty. I blink until I see him lying there.

"Brice."

He moans a little.

"Brice," I repeat, again only getting a mumble from him.

"*Brice*!" I scream finally.

"Huh, what?" He snaps upright. "Uh, I feel… actually"—he breaths deeply—"I feel better."

"I know what you mean." I smile. "Like you're a little more *yourself*."

He smiles back at me.

"So we just do this seven more times?" he asks.

"I guess." I look over at Jesus, but He's busy fixing a chair. I don't think we'll get much help at the moment.

"You don't need it." Jesus smiles, not looking away from His project.

"Okay." I look around. "Who's next?" I might as well go to the source.

My seven remaining demons all perk up a little bit, though at different speeds. I scan them thoughtfully.

"What about you, little one?" I ask, looking at the large one with teal eyes. "Might as well go big," I add.

"Are they the same for both of us?" he asks. "What the color of their eyes mean?"

"I guess so," I respond. "That's indifference. Jesus said—"

"It's the worst sin of our age," we say together and laugh.

"Good to know we're on the same page," he says. "Have at it." He motions for me to start.

"Come here," I coax it over to me, making kissy noises.

It looks at me nonchalantly but does edge its way to me, step by step. When it is close enough, I scoop it up in my arms.

"Your turn," I say sweetly as if it was a pet.

I sit back and lift it onto my knees. I look deeply into its eyes.

"Okay," I say. "I accept you." I try to recreate the first experience. I close my eyes and open up to the creature and…

Nothing happens.

I open my eyes and look at it, but it just yawns and looks at its claws, bored. I look up at Brice where he is crouching a few feet away.

"It isn't working," I say.

He shrugs his shoulders. "What did you do the last time?"

"I was laying down," I say, switching positions to mimic the first attempt. "It came up to me, so it was here"—I set the demon in about the same spot as the first one—"and I said… what was it?"

Brice shrugs.

"Do… do you want to go back?" My voice quivers, unsure.

Indifference yawns at me and still looks bored.

"I don't think it wants to go anywhere," Brice jokes.

I sit up, frustrated.

"I don't know, it was like the other one wanted to become a part of me again," I say, exasperated.

"It did because you truly understood it and accepted it."

Brice and I both jump.

I look at Jesus, who is now standing much closer.

"So I need to... to understand each one and accept it," I say, trying to talk my way through what He said.

"Yeah." Jesus nods, wiping His hands clean on a rag. It is the first time I really take a good look since His resurrection, eh—the latest one. I carefully look for familiar details only to be disappointed. Nothing about His appearance is the same. He looks more like a church's handyman, with His tool belt and work clothes, than the Savior we worship here. And yet it is clearly still the same man.

"It's really me," He says, giving me a smile and returning the rag to His tool belt.

"Does it matter what we start with?" Brice butts in. "Which demon was it the first time?" He's scanning the inky creatures and I guess He's trying to match their eyes with the sin.

"Lust," I say, embarrassed.

Brice looks at me like he wants to say something, but is changing his mind. "What's... I mean, what did you connect with?"

I look down. "The part about doing *anything* to be loved. I just... I know I'm not always that loveable." My mouth goes dry.

"I can relate to that," Brice says and gives me a kind smile. Suddenly his demeanor changes. "I think I remember..." He looks at me with pain in his eyes. "Someone hurt you, didn't they? Someone you—you wanted to love you?"

Tears fill my eyes. "Yes."

I can see he is thinking hard, but some connections I can only make for myself.

"It wasn't my fault," I start.

"Oh, I didn't mean—"

"I know," I interrupt him. "Let me finish. Please."

He nods.

"I wasn't *asking* for it or anything, but—yeah I was there because I wanted to be loved so I"—I sigh—"I understand that part of me. It took a lot to get over it."

"I think I saw you with him," Brice says to me.

"I—was there more I could have done? I don't think I could have fought him."

"No," I chuckle a little, "but you didn't have to. Men can either be flashlights or cockroaches."

Brice looks puzzled at my metaphor, so I continue, "Don't worry, you're not a cockroach, you're a flashlight. All you need to do is turn your light on the cockroaches to send them scurrying away. Sometimes I think you did that." I look up at Jesus. "But yeah, that part of me is healed."

Jesus smiles back and I am filled with joy. He's smiling because He's proud of me. I savor it, but I have work to do. I look at the creatures scattered a few feet in front of me and ponder.

"So not that one yet, but maybe…" I put the teal-eyed goblin down and I move to my hands and knees to reach the one with one blue eye. "What do you say? You ready?" I pick it up gently.

Sloth yawns and smiles at me.

"I get laying around doing nothing even if someone needs me."

"What about taking time for yourself though?" Brice asks.

"Not the same thing," I say matter-of-factly. "Sloth is more... avoiding responsibility," I say, but then add, "I think." And look at Jesus.

He smiles and says, "Sounds about right." He looks through some tools in a toolbox.

I frown. "Should we help you?" I ask Him.

"Not yet." He doesn't look up. "You're taking care of what you need." He looks up finally, adding, "We'll tackle the big rebuilding when you're ready."

I take a deep breath and get down low again. I say to the one big blue eye, "You ready?"

It yawns, but nods.

BRICE

There is another blinding light. It's blue this time and I close my eyes when I first see it. In a few seconds, it's over and I open my eyes again. I look around and realize my blue-eyed demon is gone too. I must have been healed the same time Catherine was. Speaking of, where is Catherine? She is laying on her stomach, her head resting on her folded arms. She breathes deeply, looking peaceful, angelic even.

"Yeah, you probably should wake her though," Jesus says. "You're just getting to the good stuff." He points at me with a hammer.

"Hey," I say and gently shake her shoulder. She mumbles and moves her head face down.

I try again a little more forceful. "Hey, Catherine."

She jerks her head up, and gasps, "What?"

Then recognition dawns on her. "It worked?" she asks.

"It seems so," I respond. "My turn, I guess." I scan the critters. "What about you?" I say to the one with orange eyes, but it scurries away to hide behind Catherine.

"I think that one's mine," she laughs.

I look again and spot another one with orange eyes. "Are you mine?" I ask it.

It approaches me and nuzzles against my knee. "Yep, found mine." I laugh. "Orange... which one was that again?" I ask.

Catherine sits back, thinking. Her orange-eyed demon looks at her and rises up on its back legs, mouth open.

"Is it begging?" I ask. "You did make yours into pets."

She gives me a sideways smile, then exclaims, "Oh, it's gluttony, that's why it's begging!"

I wrack my brain for a minute, then humbly ask her, "What's gluttony again?"

"It's overeating." She looks thoughtful for a moment, then continues, "Like greed, but with food."

"It's more than that," Jesus pipes up suddenly.

"Oh," I say, hoping He'll elaborate.

He smiles and continues, "It's about not having a healthy relationship with food." He pauses thoughtfully before continuing, "Food isn't a bad thing in and of itself. You're right being greedy and wasteful with it is bad. Using it to forget feeling bad isn't great either. Depriving yourself of it is a problem, too, though." He quickly adds, "But a good meal is a treat. It's fine to indulge in a moment of joy. Sharing it with another person is even better, healing in its own way."

"Okay," I say. "I don't... I don't remember having any of those problems." I shrug.

Jesus smiles. "Sometimes it isn't just about you, though it follows you. Sometimes we help someone else or don't, but they linger with us, even their demons too. We are all interconnected."

I think about what He said and about what memories I revisited with Him. "That girl," I say, "at the food court. Did I do something wrong?"

"No, you helped Jennifer," Jesus says.

"Jennifer?" Catherine pipes up. She looks at Jesus. "Like my... my sister?" Her voice cracks a little.

"Yes," Jesus says kindly.

Tears fill her eyes. "You knew my sister? You... you helped her—Jesus said so!"

"I—I met her. We had lunch one day. She seemed like she was having a rough time," I say, trying to shrug off the sudden heroism thrust on such a simple gesture.

"Yeah, she had a lot of those," Catherine says. "Thanks... thanks for being kind to her."

"Of course," I say. I want to ask Jesus how this all ties together, but clearly, Catherine is sad. I don't want to change the subject and be insensitive.

"Jennifer had anorexia," Catherine says, surprising me by being the one to connect things for me. "She died from it. You must have met her before it was too much of an issue."

I nod, thinking about Jennifer's reluctance to eat her lunch. "She—she was very sweet and kind," I say, knowing it isn't enough. No words are enough for what Catherine is going through.

With a quivering voice, she says, "Hopefully I'll see her soon."

I smile. "Hopefully," I say and think about my Peia.

We smile at each other. "I feel like I'm finally starting to understand you," I say.

"Yeah, too bad we had to die to get here," she jokes.

We both laugh.

Something paws at my leg and I look down to see the orange-eyed demon looking up at me.

"Okay, so you're gluttony," I say to it. I pick the pot-bellied demon up and look it straight in the eyes. "And you're all about food. And you're not even really about me." I smile at it. "Are you ready to heal?"

"Wait," Catherine interjects, picking hers up, "together?"

I nod and turn back to mine.

I smile as an orange glow surrounds us. It must be working!

Chapter 23

"Lord, make me an instrument of your peace
Where there is hatred, let me sow love
Where there is injury, pardon
Where there is doubt, faith
Where there is despair, hope
Where there is darkness, light
And where there is sadness, joy
O Divine Master, grant that I may
Not so much seek to be consoled as to console
To be understood, as to understand
To be loved, as to love
For it is in giving that we receive
And it's in pardoning that we are pardoned
And it's in dying that we are born to Eternal Life
Amen"

Prayer of St Francis

CATHERINE

When I awake, we're both lying on the ground.

"Brice," I say nudging him. I want to get on with this. "*Brice!*"

"Oh hey," he says sleepily, but sitting up abruptly.

"Alright?" I ask, but I know he's fine. "We still have so many to get through," I say, "and we seem to have to talk through them or something."

"Yeah," he agrees, shaking his head to wake up more.

I breathe deeply. "My turn." I turn to the shining eyes around me. "Who's left? Indifference"—it sighs at me in reply—"is clearly last. I still have greed, envy, pride, and rage."

The golden-eyed demon rubs against my leg.

"Okay, here we go," I say to it, putting my hand out, "so when have I been greedy?"

I think of times I've passed by people in rags on the street with signs, while I sit comfortably in my car.

The demon puts a paw on my chest and I'm surrounded by a golden light.

I awake and see Brice is also on the ground with his eyes closed. It looks like he did the same thing as his creatures only have four in their ranks.

We both sit up and look at each other, but not as concerned. We're both getting used to the process.

"I guess some are easier than others," I add sitting up. I look at the moving shadows around me. "But how do we tell which are ready?"

"Good question," Brice says, shrugging. "Some seem to come to us. That's a clear sign."

I look at the one with purple eyes. "What do I need to do?" I ask it.

It strides up to me, fanning its tail and showing off.

"Yep, you're clearly pride." I look at Brice. "Time to swallow my pride?" I tease.

The demon looks at me, clearly not amused. I look at it and I look around. I spot Jesus working on rebuilding a pew.

"Um," I start, "Jesus, what exactly is pride? I mean I use the word, but I'm... I'm not sure I know when I am, or was, prideful."

"For one," He responds without looking up, "could you hold this?"

I walk over and prop up the bench of the pew for Him.

He looks at me and smiles. "It's not asking for or accepting help when you need it."

I smile at Him. "Yeah I've... I've done that." I look at Brice who has moved closer to nonchalantly be in earshot.

"It can also be when you are a little too happy with yourself. You all have room to grow. Nobody's perfect."

Brice flushes a little. "I think we all have some of both," he says, finally joining the conversation.

"What do you say we tackle it together?" I ask Brice.

"Sounds good," he says, "where's mine?" He fumbles around where the little monsters have congregated.

I look at the progress Jesus has made and wonder how long I will be here holding the pew now that I have something else to do.

He looks at me, still pounding away on the pew. "Two more nails," He answers my silent question.

"Sorry," I mumble.

"There, done." He looks at me, ignoring my apology. "Thank you for your help." He points to Brice fumbling and muttering to himself. "I think someone else needs your help now." He grabs my shoulder, tucks His chin, and looks at me intently. "Just remember you need him too."

"Okay," I respond and pick my way around the broken semi-circle where the demons have congregated.

My pride is still standing next to the chipped saint's statue, preening its feathers.

"Does yours look about the same?" I ask Brice. He looks up at mine. "More or less," he responds.

I look around. "Right here," I say and walk over to the demon who looks like a nesting peacock. As soon as I'm within arm's reach, it turns and screeches at me.

"Maybe I better," Brice says.

Brice approaches the demon and it only mildly looks annoyed at him. He picks it up and walks back to me. I turn and walk over to mine. It lets me scoop it up.

"Since this seems to knock us out or something, we should probably sit," I say, then realize how obvious that probably was as Brice is already starting to sit down.

"Yeah," is all he says.

I sit facing Brice, each of us holding the bird-like demons on our laps. We look at each other silently. The memories I have walked through with Jesus flash before me and I feel humbled. Now I see Brice in so many of them. How did I go through life not noticing how important he was to me? I wonder if he feels it too. I look down. 'It isn't love or anything,' I think as I blush.

"Actually it is love, just not the romantic kind," Jesus says, making me jump. I hadn't noticed Him approach us.

"Um… what?" Brice says.

Jesus just looks at him with one eyebrow raised.

"But not the romantic kind of love… what else is there?" Brice asks Him thoughtfully.

"There is a whole world full of love that isn't romantic," Jesus responds.

BRICE

I'm sitting with what is apparently my pride in my lap, seriously rethinking nearly every decision in my life.

"So we… love each other?" Catherine asks Jesus.

"What's not to love?" Jesus smiles jokingly. "Besides, *I* am love. I'm at the heart of every relationship. When you come together, I am more myself too." He smiles.

246

I turn back to the creature on my lap and scratch under its beak. It makes an eerie sort of cooing noise.

"So to accept our pride, we need to understand when and why we didn't ask for or accept help and also when we thought too highly of ourselves," I say, trying to refocus.

I look up at Catherine. "I'm sorry. I…"

"I know," she says. "I'm sorry too, I didn't know either…"

The teal-eyed demons screech at us.

"Apparently not the time," I laugh.

CATHERINE

There is a flash of purple and we are left crumpled over again. At least we're still sort of sitting still. Maybe this is getting easier.

'*Time to move on*,' I think as I look at the green-eyed goblin.

"Envy…" I ponder my life for a while. "I mean I know I'm not above envy, but I… I can't think of any specific…" I let my voice trail off.

"What about picking on people? Some people say *that* comes from envy, and you weren't exactly the nicest kid…"

I look at him crossly, but he's probably right.

"Yeah, sometimes, I guess." I look away.

"Isn't it better to face it?" Brice says smugly.

"You know you can be annoying sometimes?" Then I soften. "Sometimes, it's when you're right."

I look at my green-eyed monster and begin, "I envied… people who seemed to have it easy."

Brice raises one eyebrow quizzically. Apparently, this is not what he expected.

"I probably need to be more specific, hmmm. Okay, I envy people... I know!" I begin again, "There was this one girl..." I don't want to admit it was the girl he ended up marrying. "She... she had it easy, okay? Her parents... just loved her. Everyone did. She didn't have to *earn* it. She— she just glowed. She didn't have to be perfect."

Compassion fills Brice's eyes, replacing his smugness. Maybe I'm being too hard on him by calling it smugness.

"You don't have to be perfect," he croons.

"She seemed to have everything I wanted," I say softly. "She—she was respected"—my voice cracks—"at a time I wasn't."

"Maybe you weren't respecting yourself?" Brice interjects.

"You think I haven't heard that?" I snap and he actually jumps back a little.

"Sorry," I say half-heartedly. "I—okay, so I just wasn't really taught it... I guess..."

Brice looks at me puzzled.

"I was told 'I'm special' but I..." I turn away. "I didn't feel valued. All I ever heard was that I needed to be better."

Brice's shoulders drop.

"I wasn't really valued," I quickly move on, "not until Tim, my husband." I look up at Brice. "Before that, no one treated *me* the way you treated Sophie."

BRICE

I'm shocked at Catherine's words, but the emerald glow swallows her up before I can respond. When my vision clears again, I'm not sure if it's okay to bring it up. I mean we are moving past stuff. Better not to open old wounds.

"I see that Jesus is nearly finished rebuilding the pews. It is odd to see the different woods in combination, but it's beautiful."

'Everything is coming together,' I think hopefully.

"Your turn," Catherine says. "What about that one?" She points to the one with pink eyes. "Isn't it *lust*?" she teases.

"Oh, no it's not like that," I say firmly.

"I know, just teasing," she says. "It's about what you'd do for love." Her voice is serious and brittle.

I look at it. "Okay, but I've—there's a lot I won't do. Even for love."

The pink-eyed demon approaches me and when I don't object, it cuddles into my lap, purring.

"I don't think that's the point," Catherine says, a little condescendingly. "It's not about that line, it's about… loneliness," she finishes sadly.

"Sometimes anything is better than being alone," I say, thinking more about Catherine than myself.

"Exactly." She half-smiles at me.

I look back into the rosy eyes and am relieved when the warm light consumes me.

Chapter 24

"Come back to me with all your heart
Don't let fear keep us apart
Trees do bend though straight and tall
So must we to others' call

Long have I waited for
Your coming home to me
And living deeply our new lives"

Hosea (Come Back to Me) by John
Michael Talbot

CATHERINE

"This is working," I say to Brice, "only a few left. What's next?"

The big one with red eyes walks up to me.

"This one should be easy. I mean I don't go storming around raging at everyone!"

It looks up at me and smiles a toothy grin.

I sit down and look it straight in the eyes. I take a deep breath and…

Nothing happens.

I think about a time I snapped at my husband. I think about yelling at a bad driver, I even think about fighting with my sister. I take another long deep breath.

Nothing happens. Again.

"It isn't working," Brice says, stating the obvious. The crimson eyes in front of me blaze. "I know," I whisper to it.

I sit back, looking for some helpful advice.

Jesus is piecing together another pew, but smiling, He walks over to me.

"Even I got angry," He says when He stretches out next to me. "There's more in you though. The real stuff you need to face. Who are you angry at? Really?"

"I'm…" I let out a sigh. "I'm angry at Theodore."

"Clearly." Jesus smiles.

"I'm angry at my mom, for being distant," I say carefully. "I mean she wasn't that bad, but—"

Jesus raises His hand to stop me. "Try to stay with it, not explain it away."

"I'm…" I sigh, exasperated. "I'm a woman, I… I'm not supposed to get angry," I mumble.

"But you do," Jesus corrects.

"Yes." I stare blankly at nothing in front of me.

"Me too," Brice butts in.

"It's not the same." I roll my eyes at him.

"I know," he says.

I look at him and my heart swells with compassion.

"Well you do always have to be the 'nice guy,'" I say. "Rage isn't a part of being 'nice.' As a woman, I always have to be 'nice,' too."

Brice looks at his own scarlet-eyed gargoyle. "Let's stop being nice, together." He looks up directly into my eyes.

"Together," I respond.

I look back at my rage a little more determined. "I'm"—my voice still quivers—"I'm mad at advertisements that try to make me feel bad."

"I'm mad at getting fired from my dad's dream job for me."

I look at Brice. "I'm mad that your dad had a dream job for you!" I continue. "I'm mad at my ex for being a jerk!"

"I'm mad at my mom for not accepting my faith."

"I'm mad at guys who catcall."

"I am too," Brice yells, and we both laugh.

"I'm mad about my miscarriage"—my voice cracks a little, but I continue—"and what you did at the pharmacy."

Brice stiffens, but continues, "I'm mad at you for picking on my wife when she was younger."

"I am, too, at myself." I fumble for the words. I regroup and add, "I'm mad at Jennifer for dying."

"I'm mad at my daughter's cancer for taking her."

"I'm mad I died of cancer." A single tear streams out of my eye, exposing my pain.

"I'm mad at getting hit by a drunk driver!" Brice yells. "By *your* friend!"

"I'm furious you didn't save me!"

"I…" His face falls. "I am, too."

"I'm… I'm mad I didn't stop Tony," I say, deflated.

A ruby glow begins and spreads, consuming both of us.

When I open my eyes, I am crumpled over and I smile when I see Brice is too.

"We're almost there," I whisper.

He opens his eyes. "I know." He smiles.

BRICE

I'm still sitting up this time when I open my eyes, albeit leaning against a pew. I am relieved when I see that Catherine is still sitting, too. All the pews are fixed and it looks like Jesus is sweeping up with a broom. The walls and ceiling are still a mess.

"We're almost there," she whispers.

"I know," I say, smiling.

"One left," Catherine says kindly. There is a touch of sadness in her eyes.

'*Me too*,' I think to myself.

"So what do we—I mean how do we…" I let my voice trail off.

"I know, I mean with everything else…" Catherine says. Then she blurts out, "I'm sorry. Really, I am. You—you didn't have to die and…" She looks down. "I'm sorry."

"Me too." I take her hand. "I'm sorry I wasn't there for you too and"—I look down, then up at Jesus, who has just come up the aisle—"can… can I see her again?"

"You won't need to. For a while. There's more work to be done first." He points at a broken wall. My heart sinks.

"So we aren't going to fix it together?" Catherine asks. "I mean this is kind of *our* space now."

"It is," Jesus says, "and you both need to add to it and fix it more, even tear a few more things apart first, but in the end, it'll still be yours. It'll be even more yours. Bigger. Big enough for you to let everyone in."

Catherine and I lean against the pews in silence. I don't want to say goodbye and it looks like she doesn't want to either.

"Come here," Jesus says. We both walk with Him to the front of the church just before the steps. There is a hole in the ceiling above us. He lays down, stretching His legs out toward the steps, and motions us to follow suit. We lay down and position our heads together so our bodies stretch out like spokes on a wheel below the dark opening. I gasp when I see stars brighter and clearer than I have ever seen twinkling above us. The three of us lie there and gaze at the wonder above us.

"It's beautiful," Catherine says, but mostly the three of us just stare at the sky above. My breath slows and I find a deep, quiet peace welling up inside of me.

As I lay there under the stars it dawns on me, "where two or three are gathered in my name..." I whisper.

"Yes," Jesus says, "there am I in their midst, but not like this. Like this." He lifts His hands and it seems like He throws a shower of fireflies above us. The twinkling lights hover above us for a moment then align in an intricate, lacey, pattern between Catherine and myself from heart to heart.

"What—" Catherine starts to say, but stops to take in the beauty between us.

"Love," Jesus says, "when you gather in my name, the love between you, that's where I am."

254

We all smile at each other for a little while.

"But this isn't where you both will stay," Jesus finally says breaking the silence as the twinkling lights fade away.

Catherine looks at me again, excited, then back at the stars pointing. I follow her gesture to a rosy twinkling star. "Pretend that one's me."

"Okay," I say.

"And that bluish one right next to it? That's you." I get it, but she continues, "Then as we keep healing, we just need to look up and know we're not really that far apart."

I smile. "I like that."

We all fall silent again.

Finally, Jesus says, "Now I think you're ready."

We all stand up and look at each other. I look around at our merged chapels around us. "But—" I begin.

"You don't have to say goodbye. Not really," Jesus says. "You never have to say goodbye again." He points to my heart. "She is in you as I am in you. The same goes for you, Catherine. Brice is right there with you. You will each move on step by step until all is made new again."

"But how? It's now one chapel," I ask.

"It is and it will be duplicated so you each can continue to grow as you need to, and keep combining with all the people from your own lives," Jesus explains.

"All?" There is a change in Catherine's voice that makes the hair on the back of my neck stand on end. "I'll—I'll have to…" She doesn't finish, but I understand who she's talking about.

I leap to her defense. "Can't I go with her? No, really, go to… to protect her. She shouldn't have to face him, whoever he is, alone!"

"And she won't. She will have you with her and everyone else she encounters before she faces him, each time getting stronger. Neither of you will ever really be alone again, but…" Jesus is looking at a stained glass window shaped like a heart. He turns to me again and adds, pointing to a stain still on my tunic, "You both have more work to do."

He looks up into Catherine's eyes and says kindly, "More healing to do."

I look around and wonder how many other chapels we will add to this one, but I will just have to find out.

We don't have to look for the last two demons; they have found us and are pawing to be picked up.

I look at Catherine and smile. She looks at me and smiles back. "Good, you can be someone else's pain in the keester," she mocks.

"Ready?" I ask, but the only response is a blue-green light that engulfs us both.

THE END

FOR NOW…

[1] Crosby, Alfred W. The Measure of Reality: Quantification and Western Society, 1250-1600. Cambridge University Press. Cambridge, UK. 1997

[2] Lama, Dalai. Dalai Lama's Little Book of Wisdom. Illustrated, Hampton Roads Publishing, 2010.

Thank you so much for reading my book! I hope you enjoyed it. My goal in writing is that people can say they look at something about the world, their faith, or even themselves differently after reading my work.

Look for more exciting titles yet to come!

I would sincerely like your feedback and anything you have to share. You can contact me directly at creationsbycarolecurry@gmail.com. How can I make this book and future books better?

Will you leave a quick review on Amazon?

Share your thoughts, even if it is brief.

About the Author

Carole has a bachelor's degree in psychology and one in religious studies from the University of Wyoming. She works for a non-profit and enjoys mountain life in Wyoming with her husband, kids, and dog. Carole loves cooking, drawing, painting, singing, and any other creative outlet she can pick up. She loves trying to bring to life whatever her imagination dreams up. Carole is passionate about her faith and attends a Catholic parish. She is driven by the hope that others will connect with the characters in her stories and not only gain deeper insights, but find renewed hope in their lives.

Learn more at www.*creationsbycarolecurry.com.*

Made in the USA
Coppell, TX
02 March 2021

51104819R00156